W9-ABB-933

STEEL
GUITAR

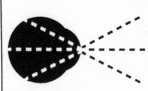

This Large Print Book carries the
Seal of Approval of N.A.V.H.

STEEL GUITAR

LINDA BARNES

Thorndike Press • Thorndike, Maine

Library of Congress Cataloging in Publication Data:

Barnes, Linda.
   Steel guitar / Linda Barnes.
      p. cm.
   ISBN 1-56054-391-4 (alk. paper : lg. print)
   1. Large type books. I. Title.
[PS3552.A682S74   1992]   92-4191
813'.54—dc20   CIP

"Among School Children" by W. B. Yeats reprinted with permission of Macmillan Publishing Company from *The Poems of W. B. Yeats: A New Edition,* edited by Richard J. Finneran. Copyright 1928 by Macmillan Publishing Company, renewed 1956 by Georgie Yeats.

"Old Friends" Words and music by Mary McCaslin. © Folklore Music/ASCAP. Reprinted by permission.

"Steel Guitar" (Danny O'Keefe) © 1970 Cotillion Music Inc. & Burdette Music. All Rights Reserved. Used by permission.

Thorndike Press Large Print edition published in 1992 by arrangement with Delacorte Press, a division of Bantam Doubleday Dell Publishing Group, Inc.

Cover design by Sean Pringle.

The tree indicium is a trademark of Thorndike Press.

This book is printed on acid-free, high opacity paper.

Singers come and go; the music business waxes and wanes. The blues are popular and unpopular, often at the same time. The blues artists who appear as characters in this book are creations of the author's imagination. I have surrounded them with names familiar to blues fans — names like Rory Block, Chris Smither, and the late Reverend Gary Davis — but no Dee Willis exists. Any resemblance between my characters and actual living persons is purely coincidental.

Once again, my thanks to the illustrious, if somewhat altered, reading committee: James Morrow, Susan Linn, Richard Barnes, and Ann Sievers. Chris Smither provided insight into the music scene: all the correct information is his; all errors are my own. I'm grateful to Linda Kalver for introducing me to the man who played "Miss Gibson" and to Maxine Aaronson for her legal expertise. Oh, and Roz would like me to thank the ever-vigilant T-shirt squad: John Hummel, Cynthia Mark-Hummel, and Michelle Forsythe.

My agent, Gina Maccoby, continues to watch over Carlotta's affairs with tender care, and I would also like to commend my editor, Brian DeFiore, for his humor, patience, and criticism.

*"Remember old friends we've made along the
  way,
The gifts they've given stay with us every day."*

"Old Friends"
Mary McCaslin
1977

In loving memory of

Peter Haber
H. Wesley Brinkley
Dennis Schuetz

*"She could put it all together on a real,
on a steel guitar."*

"Steel Guitar"
Danny O'Keefe

"O chestnut tree, great-rooted blossomer,
Are you the leaf, the blossom, or the bole?
O body swayed to music, O brightening glance,
How can we know the dancer from the dance?"

"Among School Children"
William Butler Yeats
1927

CHAPTER ONE

"Men darf lebn un lozn lebn," my mother always used to tell me when I was a child. Now that I'm grown I know the words translate roughly to "Live and let live," but for Mom it meant "Don't mix in."

Her warning didn't take. That's how I make my living, mixing in.

Amend that. It's how I'd make my living if I could. But the investigations business is dicey: sometimes I turn away three clients in a single day; sometimes I go for weeks without hearing a knock at my door. Because I like to eat — and I prefer to say no to the occasional client who thinks he can buy what's not for sale — I pilot a cab nights to make ends meet.

I enjoy night driving. I like the garish after-midnight world. Its clarity excites me — the glare of headlights, the flashing neon, the sharp edges. But sometimes, blinded by the glitter, I forget to pay attention to the shadows.

I was dozing at a cab stand, fanning myself with the travel section of the *Globe*. The air conditioner was going full blast; a faint stream of tepid air trickled through the vents, no match for the August heat. I was dreaming about my next fare, a well-built gentleman who'd drop miraculously into the backseat and say, "Cape Cod, please. A slow drive along the seashore, catch some ocean breeze."

Even half asleep, I recognized her.

She wore dark glasses and a cape that looked like it was made of raincoat material. Just the thought of its weight made me shudder. But for the Boston cabbie dress code, I'd have been wearing shorts, a halter, and sandals. As it was, I had on my lightest-weight khaki slacks, a thin white cotton shirt, and sneakers.

Hesitating under the hotel canopy, she groped in her shoulder bag and slipped the doorman a bill. From the way he clicked his heels and raised his whistle to his lips, what he'd just palmed was no portrait of George Washington. I gunned the motor automatically. I was the next cab in line.

For a pulsebeat, I felt like flooring it, racing away without a backward glance. Then the sweating gold-braided attendant seized the door handle, and it was too late.

I've kept track of her through the years, my old buddy Dee Willis. Hauled my black-and-white TV out of the closet to watch her that time she appeared on *Letterman*. She was so drunk they only let her sing one song at the end, and then she forgot half the words.

That must have been five years ago, and the fans have long since forgiven her. Lately her name crops up in the *Globe* every other day. *Change Up*, the album that went double platinum, or whatever they call the best there is in the record biz, in two days, or two weeks, or something incredible, had turned her into an overnight success after sixteen years.

I opened my mouth to say hello.

She didn't even glance at me. "Take me to the library," she demanded, her voice low and tense. "No. Forget it. Just cruise around Copley Square, okay? Into the South End."

I closed my mouth and bit my lower lip, nodding to let her know I'd heard. My fares generally want to go from here to there, and heaven help the jockey who detours a block out of the way.

Two blocks passed. I cranked down the front window and enjoyed the breeze. She didn't say anything. I didn't say anything. I felt awkward. It's hard to identify yourself right off the bat to an old friend who's made better than good. Especially when you're the one driving the hack.

I concentrated on squeezing through the yellow light at St. James, tailing a dark blue Mercedes. Maybe, even if she deigned to look, she wouldn't recognize me. At night, especially when I'm wearing a slouch cap over my red hair, most of my fares hardly notice I'm a woman. And my best disguise isn't the hat; it's the job. Nobody notices cab drivers.

I sneaked a look in the rearview mirror. Dee had removed the sunglasses. She seemed absorbed in the study of a painted fingernail.

The South End wasn't even a mile from her hotel, hardly a decent walk, much less a cab ride. I toyed with the idea of saying "Chintzy fare," starting things rolling with a joke. The more I hesitated the harder it got, like chatting with somebody at a party, somebody you know pretty well, but whose name you've forgotten. If you confess right off, it's not too bad. But the longer you talk, the harder it gets to ask for a name. You keep wondering who the hell you're talking to, and hoping you won't blow it.

We hit a red light and I did some more rearview-mirror gazing. The backseat was pretty dark, but a streetlamp helped. Dee was staring into space, drumming her fingers on her thigh, clutching her big shoulder bag. She looked good, maybe a little hard, but good. She unbuttoned her cape, revealing a red shirt, embroidered with enough gold thread to catch the light. I couldn't make out the pattern. She wore a long rope of gold beads and dangling, flashy earrings. Thick eyeliner, heavy-duty makeup. Maybe she'd played a gig tonight.

I hadn't noticed an ad in the newspaper, but some days I just skim it before taking it home to line the parakeet's cage.

Her wild dark hair was permed into a halo. I knew she was older than I am, but you couldn't prove it by her appearance.

We sped two blocks, got caught at another traffic light. She drew in a deep breath, held it, and let it out audibly. Then she closed her eyes and repeated the heavy-breathing business. She hadn't cranked down the back window. In her cape, she was probably melting.

I wondered where she was heading, cruising the South End in the wee hours, wondered if the encounter might not be embarrassing for both of us.

I met Dee Willis my first year at U.Mass.-Boston, jamming at a party, her pure vocals rising over a flood of badly tuned instruments, making everybody sound twice as good. She wasn't all that pretty, and she sure wasn't school-smart — but she had that voice, and in my crowd we forgave her everything for a song.

I turned onto Pembroke Street. "You want me to circle the block?" I asked, my voice barely loud enough to penetrate the square porthole in the required-by-Boston-law bulletproof divider.

"Keep going. I'll tell you where to stop."

15

She pressed her nose against the left rear window. Maybe she'd stopped looking at people in general, not just cabbies. I've heard celebrities get like that, pretending to wear blinders so they won't have to answer stupid questions all the time, or get interrupted by autograph hounds during meals.

I tried the rearview mirror again, but this time edged a bit to my right, so my own reflection stared back at me. Dee looked like she was doing fine. And me? Not bad, thank you. If I pick up a couple more skip traces a year, I might be able to give up cabbing altogether.

My trouble-sensing radar blipped as we crossed Tremont and kept on traveling into one of the city's less savory neighborhoods.

Dee rapped on the shield. "Hang a left," she said. I obliged. She seemed to be navigating from memory.

"Stop here!" She shoved money through the little sliding window. A bill fluttered to the seat and I bent to get it. By the time I'd straightened up, she was slamming the door.

Where was she going? We hadn't stopped near any restaurants that might be open this late. She raced across a lane of traffic into a small neighborhood park.

The park, sometimes called Blackstone Square, sometimes less pleasant names, is a pretty safe place to hang out during the day if you don't mind winos bumming a dollar. At night, Bostonians give it a wide berth, frightened by the homeless with their grapes-of-wrath faces.

I started up, then slowed way down. If Dee was trying to score some coke solo, things were tighter in the music world than I expected.

It wasn't hard to keep her in sight. She hurried across a deserted basketball court. The few scraggly trees hung limply in the heat. A triple-decker apartment briefly blocked my view as I turned the corner.

Dee seemed to be cruising the grassy center of the park, chatting with bench-squatters. I pulled the cab into a fireplug slot and watched, puzzled.

I was a cop for six years. I know what a drug buy looks like.

Dee held a level hand above her head as if she were describing something big. Moonlight caught the side of her face. She nodded, then pulled a crumpled bill out of her bag, gave it to the figure on the bench, and moved along.

That part looked familiar, the transfer of cash, but Dee didn't seem to get what she wanted in exchange for the currency.

I yanked off my cap, lifted the heavy curls

off the nape of my neck, and wished I'd brought along an elastic band and a few hairpins.

Dee repeated the performance at another bench. A ragtag guy with a week's worth of beard started following her. She turned and spoke to him. I flicked off the air conditioner's useless belch, but all I could hear was a babel of voices. The man's carried farther, but I couldn't understand the words.

Another guy lumbered over, and this one looked like major trouble. Drunk or stoned, he was big and unsteady on thick legs, and seemed to be wearing his entire wardrobe, shirts layered over shirts, pants over pants.

Heat alone can cause ugly moods. Add alcohol or drugs and you've got one of the reasons cops hate hot August nights.

I heard an angry cry and cut the ignition, shoving the keys into my pocket. The cry was followed by a scream. I was already out of the cab and racing toward the park.

I'd automatically grabbed the foot-long chunk of lead pipe I keep beneath the seat. It wasn't as comforting as my service revolver used to be.

"Hell, you can afford it, lady," a man's voice shouted as I approached.

Dee's hand was tight on the strap of her shoulder bag. She was staring down a guy a foot taller than she was, and she didn't look half as frightened as she should have been. Maybe she didn't see the people gathering on the asphalt playground.

"Get lost," I heard her say, arrogant as ever. "It's none of your business."

"Throw the bag here, bitch," the over-dressed drunk yelled. He was leaning on the edge of a trash bin, too soused to move, and for that I was grateful. He egged the others on, their self-appointed cheerleader.

From the direction of the playground a steady stream of hungry, shaky, drunken souls moved toward Dee like sharks closing on a bleeding fish. Her cape swung open and her shirt glittered in a car's passing beams.

I called her name.

She didn't hear me. Another guy, mid-fifties with a tuft of white hair, made a swipe at her bag and connected. They started playing tug-of-war, and the shoulder strap broke. Dee got a corner of the purse and yanked, but the bag upended and spilled with a soft cascade of thuds and clunks. The man hit the ground with a grunt, grasping for change, bills, pawn-able trinkets.

I pushed my way between two women muttering at the edge of the pack and shoved in close enough to grab Dee's shoulder.

"Leave me alone," she said, fighting me,

clinging to her handbag. Then she looked up at me for the first time. I saw the shock of recognition in her eyes.

"Let's get out of here," I said firmly.

"She's gonna give us ten bucks apiece," a man hollered.

"Shit," I muttered under my breath. Passing out free cash on the ritziest corner in Boston will get you a guaranteed unpleasant situation. Playing Santa where ten bucks will buy a lot of wine or a lid of dope is just plain stupid. Before my eyes, the promise of free money was changing a handful of unfortunates into a mob.

As I started hauling Dee toward the cab, I could feel sweat trickle down my back. I heard a bottle break behind me.

"Move it," I urged. She was hanging back, staring over her shoulder. Somebody made a dive for her beads.

"I know him," a deep voice yelled from the dark. "Gimme the ten."

"Me too."

"Where's the money, lady?"

"I see the bastard all the time."

"I seen him, lady."

There were at least ten of them circling, four blocking us from the cab. Another bottle broke and this time it was no accident. The jagged lip of a beer bottle caught the sleeve of Dee's shirt. She gasped. I struck out with my pipe and heard an answering growl of surprise and pain.

"Toss your bag over their heads," I ordered Dee, "and run for the cab. I'll hold them off."

She grabbed at her arm and I wondered if the glass had cut her badly. The handbag fell in front of her, its broken strap snaking toward the crowd. Her beads got another tug and broke, spilling on the patchy grass. I kept her from diving after them. I was afraid if I knelt to retrieve the handbag, the pack would pile on top of me.

I swung the pipe in a circle to clear some space. A bottle glanced off my shoulder and I whirled to face a nonexistent antagonist.

I was breathing hard. With effort, I slowed it down.

"Okay," I said loudly, using my cop voice. "Clear a path. Me and the lady are walking away. Whatever you find on the ground, you keep. Fair deal, okay?" I had Dee by the wrist. She struggled feebly. I had forgotten how small she was. My right hand clutched the chunk of pipe. It had felt cool when I'd first grabbed it; now it felt as sticky and damp as my palm.

"What about my ten bucks?" the drunk leaning on the trash can said loudly.

"On the ground," I said. "Party's over."

"Don't let 'em go till you see money," somebody advised with sodden wisdom. "They got jewelry? Diamonds?"

"You been watching too much TV," I said, edging closer to the cab, waving the pipe. "Everybody's rich on TV. Me, I drive a hack."

"Yeah, what about rich bitch here?"

"She dropped her jewelry. You're stepping on it."

A couple of the truly stoned sank to all fours, but the rest weren't fooled. I ran my tongue over my dry upper lip. I wasn't sure I could talk my way out without cracking somebody hard with the pipe — and I didn't know who might have a knife, or a cheap gun. I was scanning the crowd at hand level, looking for the flash of metal, when the cruiser turned the corner.

There's a time for self-reliance and a time to yell for help.

I screamed my lungs out, and the siren's answering wail never sounded so good.

22

CHAPTER TWO

Dee hadn't been afraid of the gang, but she was terrified of the cops. Now *she* grabbed *my* arm and tried to yank me toward the cab. The pack dispersed in the direction of the basketball court. The chunk of lead pipe suddenly felt heavy, so I lowered my arm and concentrated on breathing. The back of my shirt was soaked with sweat. Dee tugged at my sleeve again, but I shook her off.

A cop so young he had to be a rookie burst out of the charging unit and collared a drunk — definitely not one of the ringleaders, who all seemed to have melted into the misty heat. The cop pretzeled his captive into a choke hold and marched him close enough that I could smell him.

"This guy rob you girls, or what?" he yelled, adrenaline raising his voice a hundred decibels.

Calling me "girl" while I had a length of pipe in my hand was a dumb move. His second dumb move was presuming he knew the score. *Never anticipate,* they taught me at the academy. No assumptions. Your opening line is always *What's going on?*

23

"Let's get out of here," Dee muttered. She tried to whisper, but the words blared.

"What's the hurry?" the cop said in a less sympathetic tone. "You got some ID on you?"

"This your bag?" The rookie's partner, a black woman with high-piled graying hair, pulled Dee's battered handbag out from under a bush.

"Yeah, uh, no," Dee said, swallowing and sounding like she'd been practicing all her life to be a suspect.

"Maybe we ought to go back to the station and see if we can sort this out," the male cop said, relaxing his grip on the sputtering drunk.

"No," Dee said too quickly. "No. I, uh, was taking a cab, and uh, we got lost. Stopped to ask directions. No trouble. No problem."

The drunk, a wiry coffee-colored individual who could have been any age from twenty to fifty, picked that moment to stagger, point a shaky finger at Dee, and blurt, "She steal money, that bitch. She steal my ten dollar. I make charge."

"Carlotta," Dee whispered urgently, proving beyond a doubt that she remembered my name, "can't you do something, for chrissake? Please?"

Now I don't generally take to the role of rescued damsel, but I had been genuinely pleased to see these particular cops. Initially, I'd felt a sense of camaraderie, a desire to slap hands and commend them for a job well done. My enthusiasm melted as it became obvious that they were determined to mistake us for a couple of suburban hausfraus slumming for a dope buy. I could practically see the thought balloons over their heads as they all but ignored the homeboys and zeroed in on the two of us.

I was surprised neither of them recognized Dee. She's been on the cover of *People*.

The drunk kept shouting that Dee had robbed him, and he wanted to "make charge." English was not his primary tongue and "make charge" was about all the cops could get out of him. I did not offer to translate. The more Dee protested her innocence, the guiltier she sounded.

There was no ID in the handbag. No wallet. No money. A comb and a couple of hairpins. Picked clean.

Still, if Dee hadn't given two different names — Jane Adams the first time they asked and Joan the second — we probably wouldn't have won a free ride in a cruiser.

I backed up her story and kept quiet about her name, but I sure wished she could have dreamed up a better lie. Her tale of losing an address, losing her way, and forgetting her handbag sounded definitely fishy. As a citizen and a cabbie, capable of proving it with my driver's license, my private investigator's photostat, and other assorted paper, I could have walked. But I hung around; I wanted to see how Dee slid out of it. I was also curious as to why she'd gotten into it. And she was gripping my arm so hard, I wasn't sure I could escape.

I don't get many chances to ride in the rear seat of a cruiser anymore. I'd forgotten such amenities as the lack of inside door-handles. Three in the back was a definite crowd. I hoped Dee's drunken accuser wouldn't vomit.

"So how've you been?" I said once we got settled behind the mesh screen, with Dee practically sitting on my lap in her effort to avoid contact with the drunk. The cruiser could have used a giant-sized can of air freshener. The drunk added nothing pleasant to the bouquet.

"Hey, I thought you just picked her up in the cab," the female cop said accusingly, pivoting her head to stare at me balefully over her shoulder.

"I did," I shot back. "I'm making light conversation."

"Carlotta," Dee murmured urgently, "can you help me out here? I just can't have this happen, you know? Can't you do something?"

26

"You're doing fine. Keep it up, you'll spend the night in a cell — " Her warning glare stopped me from using her real name.

"Isn't there some way? Weren't you a — "

"No whispering back there," the male cop warned.

"No whispering?" I repeated. "You sure that's illegal?" The drunk was praying to the Virgin in rapid-fire Spanish.

"Smart-assing isn't gonna help," Dee snapped.

She had a point. "Are you taking us to D?" I asked the cops.

"Why?"

"I wondered if you'd mind a little detour. That way I can save you some paperwork, maybe even a reprimand. Those written reprimands sure look bad when it comes time for the sergeant's exam."

I had their attention. The rookie drove more slowly. The woman peered at me through slitted eyes. I started naming names. Neither of them looked impressed until I got to Mooney.

When I was a cop I worked for Mooney. He was a sergeant then. He's a lieutenant now and unlikely to rise further through the ranks. He's too good a street cop — and too lousy an ass-kisser.

Mooney owes me, but I hate to call in favors

because the chance to help out my former boss rarely comes my way. On the other hand, Dee and I go way back, and her finally booming career probably didn't need the notoriety of a bust.

The woman cop knew Mooney. She was starting to figure out that she had something a little unusual on board. She kept staring at Dee like she was on the verge of remembering something important.

I wasn't sure if Mooney was working nights, although he has a rep for pulling rotten shifts. He lives with his mother. I've met her, and to me she's a perfect excuse to demand twenty-four-hour-a-day duty.

When Mooney is in his office, he's over at the old D Street station, since that's where they stash the homicide squad.

I tried to talk the cops into making the trip to Southie, but the male cop refused, and I couldn't really blame him.

I gave Dee an encouraging smile despite the fetid air and overcrowded conditions. There was another chance, admittedly slimmer. Mooney often worked out of Headquarters on Berkley Street. That was hardly a major detour, and I talked the woman into giving it a try.

We arrived at the station at the same time as a wagonload of hookers. One of them waved at me, but I didn't recognize her under a ratty blond wig.

I didn't recognize the desk sergeant either. He gave us scant attention, preferring the charms of the sidewalk hostesses. The woman cop finally cornered him and they held a whispered conference while Dee fidgeted and the drunk said thirty-seven Hail Marys.

"So is he in or not?" I asked when the drunk started on number thirty-eight.

"Upstairs," the woman ordered.

We tagged along behind the prostitutes. How do women manage to walk in five-inch spikes? I marveled. Maybe they're the latest in non-concealed defensive weapons.

I saw Mooney before I heard him. He just stood there, arms folded — neat striped shirt tucked into faded chinos — watching the parade. Someone must have phoned and warned him.

"New job?" he asked, tongue firmly planted in cheek. I was so glad to see him, I almost gave him an unprofessional hug. He smelled of cigarettes, having taken up the habit again after almost a year off. I gave it up ages ago, but the secondhand smoke smelled great, especially after the cruiser.

Dee had slipped on her shades and they were making her less than inconspicuous. Never wear sunglasses at night unless you want to look like a drug addict. She buttoned her cape in spite of the sweltering heat, and tried to fade into a wall.

If I was going to help her, I needed to cut her loose before some fan wised up — or worse, a jailhouse reporter. I drew Mooney into a corner and used up a good many points, promising to explain later.

If Mooney and I had met any other way, I'm sure we'd have wound up in bed by now. But for years I steeled myself against thinking about him as a possible bedmate, and by the time he finally became accessible, the chemistry just wasn't there.

Like sleeping with a brother, I tell him whenever he asks me out.

Other than my feeling that intimacy would be incestuous, I have nothing against Mooney. He's good-looking if you like them tall, solid, and Irish. He's got deceptively mild brown eyes that can freeze you with a glance. He's close to forty, but you can only tell by the fine little crinkles at the corners of his eyes. His waistline hasn't expanded.

Mooney explains our lack of romance in other terms. He says I flat out prefer outlaws to cops anyday — my current beau, Sam Gianelli, son of a Boston mob underboss, is a case in point.

Mooney said a few words to the officers

who'd brought us in and they made apologetic noises. Dee's accuser wound up with a lecture on public intoxication that he was too far gone to understand. The cops offered him a ride back to the park, which I thought was decent of them.

Mooney said he'd be more than happy to drive me and my friend. I would have opted for the smelly cruiser and a quick escape from his close scrutiny, but before I could decline, Dee said thank you in a fervent tone. Mooney hustled us out the back door and commandeered a new unit with working A/C. His old Buick is a wreck.

Dee kept her face shielded from the light, grabbed the back door handle, and ducked quickly inside. I sat up front and aimed all the vents full on my face.

We drove back to the scene of the non-crime.

Dee mumbled her thanks to Mooney as she left the car, head bent, cape fastened, dark glasses in place.

"I sure like your new stuff, Dee," Mooney said with a warm smile. He squealed the tires when he pulled away. Boys will be boys.

"Shit," Dee said, with a pleased grin, as she squeezed behind the meter into the front seat of my cab. "How'd he recognize me?"

I didn't answer because I was busy staring

at the red ticket plastered to the cab's windshield. Parking at a hydrant is a hundred-buck fine, and the cab company sure won't pay it.

Like my mother always used to say, "Don't mix in."

CHAPTER THREE

I started the motor. Dee pushed back the torn sleeve of her shirt and a thin red trickle oozed down her arm.

"Got a Kleenex or something?" she asked.

"Try the dash." My pal, Gloria, dispatcher and co-owner of the Green & White Cab Company, stocks the cabs with first-aid kits, but some of the bozos who pilot them steal anything, including Band-Aids.

Dee rummaged in silence for a while, then said, "Here's one of those things you clean your hands with after you eat Kentucky Fried Chicken."

"If it's still in the wrapper, use it," I advised.

Caught by a traffic light near the Public Garden, I watched as Dee wiped her arm and cranked down the passenger window, presumably to toss the used towelette. Instead she kept a tight grip on it, leaned back, and giggled. The sound echoed off the dividing shield.

"Something funny?" I asked.

"I was just thinking I'd probably get arrested for littering," she said. "Jesus," she gasped, squeezing out words between eruptions of laughter, "of all the cabs in all the cities in all the world . . . Is that how it goes? You know, that line from *Casablanca*. Bogie says it. 'Of all the gin joints in all the cities in all the — ' "

" 'You had to walk into mine,' " I quoted with feeling. "Calm down." Some people throw giggle-fits when they realize they won't have to spend the night in jail. Relief takes mysterious forms.

"Shit, I'm sorry, Carlotta. Not recognizing you right off, I mean. I wasn't expecting . . . What I mean" — her laughter took on a bitter, self-mocking tone — "I mean, here I go skulking out of the hotel, all incognito and anonymous, and first thing, right off, I take a cab with you at the wheel. I mean, I'm doing everything just right, you know?"

Her voice had begun to waver.

"Lose a lot of cash?" I asked.

She hesitated. I gave her a raised eyebrow and she apparently decided that saving her ass twice in a single night gave me the right to a question or two.

"Around a hundred bucks," she muttered. "Maybe two."

My eyebrow went up another notch. I know what's in my wallet down to the last dime.

"Back to the hotel?" I asked her.

"Yeah, I guess."

"You staying there? Nice place," I said.

"Remember my apartment on Mass. Ave.? What a toilet that was."

"But the parties were good," I said. You get enough people together in a one-room dive and nobody notices the decor.

We drove another three blocks. The silence grew as heavy and uncomfortable as the heat.

"Carlotta," Dee said slowly, "that license you showed the cops — are you the kind of investigator who finds people?"

"I'm a private investigator. I do missing persons work."

"Can you get rid of the cab?"

"I suppose I could," I said doubtfully.

She was suddenly eager. "Come upstairs. You can help me out. I mean, you're perfect. You're like a gift. I'll pay for your time. I'll pay for what you lose tonight with the cab. I'll pay your damn parking ticket. I mean, even if you won't do it, I'll pay."

I pulled up in front of the Four Winds. The doorman hurried down the walk, but Dee waved him off.

My hand hovered at the ignition. I straightened up and turned to look at her. I could feel my jaw muscles clench. "Is Cal with you?" I asked finally, breaking a long pause.

She looked searchingly at my face. I concentrated on a nearby traffic light.

"He left," she said. "Long time ago."

"You don't want me to find him, do you?"

"Hell, no."

CHAPTER FOUR

The first thing I noticed about the lobby was the air-conditioning; the place could have doubled as a refrigerator. I sucked in the icy air gratefully, felt my thin shirt start to stiffen and chill.

We skirted carefully composed groups of furniture facing off across Oriental rugs. I wondered if anyone dared to sit in the antique chairs. Although we were the only passengers, we didn't speak in the elevator. Dee hit the lowest button on the right. Top floor.

You know how your tongue always strays to the sore spot in your mouth? Mine does.

And add another character flaw: when I was a kid, after it rained, there was this one rock in the backyard that positively demanded to be turned over. I'd shiver a little before I did it, because I never failed to find some mushy crawly thing underneath it — but it never occurred to me not to look.

I watched the indicator lights wink the passing floors, and realized that after all this time, Cal still feels like a sore spot in my mouth, a big unturned rock in my yard. Calvin Therieux, my ex-husband. The one who left town with Dee Willis.

That's right. Waltzed off with my best friend, Dee, the woman with whom I'd sung five thousand songs and shared more than a few men. I'd layered her unruly hair and taught her how to wield a blow-dryer. She'd ironed my curls till they were fashionably straight. Dee and Cee, they called us. Dee and Carlotta, always together back then. Such a striking duo.

She had the boobs, the dimples, the Southern charm. I had the boyish ass, the long legs, the blazing red hair. We used to kid each other that we had one great body between the two of us.

And then there was Cal.

So why hadn't I deserted her in the park?

More to the point, what the hell was I doing in the elevator?

I remember taking a biology test for Dee right before she dropped out of college. My hand shook when I forged her name to the blue book. What I can't remember is why I agreed to do it.

And Cal? Well, Cal didn't really leave me for Dee, not that way, or not exclusively that way. He dropped me for cocaine, pure and simple. Dee was forming a band at the perfect time, setting out on a six-month tour. Cal had a choice: He could stay with me, get clean, get a local job; he could go with Dee, play the music, stay stoned, and party.

Uh-huh. Some choice.

The elevator door slid open.

The hallway was carpeted in wine-colored pile. The walls wore maroon-and-white-striped paper; gold-framed prints hung under brass lamps. Music poured through open double doors to the right, and from the way it stopped and started, it had to be live. Chatter mixed with the music. In the hushed lobby below, it was close to two A.M. On the eighth floor, it was party time.

"Shit," Dee muttered under her breath. "I can't believe this bash is still pumping along. MGA/America — that's my new label — flew a planeload of company stiffs out to cha-cha. Christ, I headached my way out hours ago."

She touched a conspiratorial finger to her lips and we slipped down the corridor unnoticed. She had the key in a back pocket of her tight black pants, except it was a card, not a key, which must have made it more comfy to sit on. She slipped it into a slot next to the door. A light flashed from red to green, and the door eased open when she turned the knob.

I was glad she hadn't kept the card in her handbag.

"Who's that?" a low voice demanded as we

39

entered. A woman giggled, and someone grunted and told her to shut up. The only illumination was the glow from a distant heavily-shaded lamp. Dee hit a switch and the room's size was revealed in the harsh overhead light.

At first glance it looked a little smaller than my house. The wall-to-wall was gold plush. A spray of orchids and lilies was shoved to one side of a mirrored cocktail table that separated two low ivory couches.

"Shit, Dee, you like to scare me to death." A black man wearing a Hawaiian-print shirt and Day-Glo-orange wristbands and a matching headband knelt on the carpet in front of the table. A blonde teenager, sixteen tops, sprawled next to him, blinking mascaraed lashes. Her long hair was dyed and curled to within an inch of its life, and she was wearing hot-pink tights and a lacy black thing that looked like a bra.

"Oh, great," Dee mumbled, "this is all I need."

It was a bra. A hot-pink shirt, crumpled like an exotic flower, lay on the gold rug.

"You okay, hon?" a dark-haired woman asked Dee in a raspy voice. She seemed drunk or stoned, and was supporting herself with an arm draped around a man who must have been ten years younger than she was, a thin wisp of a guy in jeans and a denim jacket. He had a slightly foreign air, dark smudgy eyes.

A bearded man was lying on the carpet, moving his arms and legs like he was making angels in the snow. Some kind of weird calisthenics, maybe. Another man was sitting on the low couch with his head in his cupped hands. All I could see was tangled sandy curls. A young woman was massaging his shoulders with practiced boredom.

"Hey," the blonde wearing the bra called, without waiting for an introduction. "I know you! You're Dee Willis! I was sure you'd come back! I'm Mimi. I'm with Freddie. And I know Hal from when he was touring with the Bow-Wows. I was with their lead guitar for practically a month."

I figured the wiry black man lining white powder on the cocktail table for either Freddie or Hal.

"Freddie plays drums," Dee said, pointing to the black man as if "drums" explained everything from snorting coke to screwing sixteen-year-olds. She tossed her cape over the back of a chair. "Brenda" — she nodded toward the dark-haired woman who'd asked after her health — "is my bass player. Why they're partying in here, I don't have the faintest. I mean, don't I get any privacy?" Dee's voice turned cooler than the air-conditioning.

"You can answer on the way out," she said.

"Lock the door, Dee," Freddie, the drummer, replied, unintimidated. "And hush up unless you want company. Who's your friend? Come on, we don't want the suits next door barging in. I don't have unlimited product, but what I do have is damn good Peruvian flake." He flashed a quick smile at Dee and deftly rolled a bill into a straw.

"Hal said use the room," the dark-haired woman offered. "He didn't exactly want us sniffing shit as a demo for the MGA execs, Dee." She was almost as tall as I am, with a stockier build. She wore wire-rimmed glasses, the old-fashioned kind, two circles connected by a bridge and held with plain earpieces. For the rest, she was round-faced, barefooted, and blue-jeaned, and looked comfortable in a sleeveless blue top. "You disappeared, and the room's perfect. Connecting door, so we don't have to stumble out in the hallway. And every once in a while we go out and make nice to the money men. The right people" — she glanced at the guy making angels on the floor as if she wasn't sure about him — "the ones who want to tank up on something that doesn't come in a glass, knock three times, then two."

Dee glanced at me speculatively. I wasn't surprised or shocked by the coke on the table, but neither was I pleased. Keep coke prices high enough so only rock stars can afford it, and I don't mind if they snort till their noses fall off.

Dee raised an eyebrow and said, "Better flush the stash, Freddie."

"Yeah, right." Day-Glo Freddie made a neat job of sniffing a line. The sixteen-year-old was untying his shoes, maybe the better to yank his pants down. And here I'd thought groupies were out of style.

I glanced at Dee. She kept a straight face while she asked, "Are you an officer of the court, Carlotta? Do you have to turn them in, or can you let them go this once?"

"Whatever you want," I said, playing along with the gag. "Up to you."

Freddie narrowed his eyes and looked cautiously from Dee to me. His tongue poked out of a corner of his mouth. He started shoveling his precious white powder into a silver cigarette case, using a six-inch metal ruler to scrape the mirrored surface clean.

The blonde giggled and pointed at me. "Forget it, Freddie. No way she's a cop."

"Freddie," Dee said warningly. "Swear to God, you're just trouble waiting to happen. I can't decide if you're gonna go down for jailbait or dope."

"Oh, preach it, Mama," Freddie chanted

sarcastically, brushing whatever powder he'd missed into a neat little line and offering the straw to the sandy-haired man on the couch. He didn't notice, but the shoulder-rubbing woman took a hit.

"Carlotta," Dee said, "would you believe he sings harmony like God's own angel? Not to mention he can keep time like a clock."

"Life isn't fair," I said.

The dark-haired woman flashed me a sloppy grin of total agreement and clung even tighter to the much younger man at her side.

"What's with you, Bren," Dee said, "encouraging this kind of shit?"

"Oh, Dee," Brenda responded in a tired whine, "come off it. You haven't been out there kissing ass all night. I've been telling everybody what a great goddamn guitar player and what a great goddamn singer you are for four freaking hours. It wears thin, you know."

"Bren, I don't set up the parties — "

"No. You just run off and leave us to pick up the pieces. Those guys expected to party with the very famous Dee Willis. Then she walks out, and they're stuck with her very un-famous bass player."

"Who'd much rather be doing other things," Freddie said with a twinkle in his voice.

"Shut the mouth, Fred. Nothing good

44

comes out of it unless you're singing," Brenda retorted.

Dee didn't seem to notice their animosity. She kept talking to the bass player. "So tell 'em you're gonna throw up, Bren. Leave. Nobody told you to be so goddamn super-responsible. Now, all of you, get out, or I'm gonna have Carlotta bust you. Show 'em your license, Carlotta."

At the word "license," Freddie stuffed his cigarette case into his girlfriend's canvas throw-all, a very streetwise thing to do, the golden rule being: Never get caught with the goods on you. He wasn't quite sure if Dee was pulling his leg or not, but he wasn't taking chances. The blonde didn't seem to realize she was holding enough to earn her a stay at MCI-Framingham.

Freddie sniffed and said, "Well, if your friend's not gonna arrest me, I been working on that bridge, that two-four A flat major shit, and you gotta hear it. You gotta tell Bren that — "

Brenda said, "Nobody's gotta tell me you're a showboat, Freddie."

"Ooh, Bren," Freddie said, a hard edge to his teasing voice, "hold tight to lover boy. You ain't gonna find a livelier specimen. Not at your age."

A knock on the connecting door, three raps,

then two, interrupted the bickering. Dee quickly crossed the carpet and stood behind the door as she edged it open.

A frowning gnomelike man walked in. I was surprised by the flood of sound that entered with him. This hotel, unlike every fleabag I've ever stayed in, had terrific soundproofing.

Dee leaned back against the door as she shut it and folded her arms deliberately across her chest. Her red shirt glittered with embroidered gold dragons. "Hal, for chrissakes, can't you keep people out of my goddamn room?"

He was in his mid-forties, maybe fifty. When he saw Dee, he started to smile, as if smiling were his natural state, but he killed the grin and spoke sternly. "You want to go out," he said flatly, "you notify me. I'll get you a driver. Okay? You want to drive around all night, fine. You come to me. You want to jog or something, I get you somebody to jog with. You don't just disappear on me. Ever."

Dee started to flare, the way she used to if you crossed her, and I braced myself for a shouting match. She surprised me by making a visible effort at self-control. She closed her eyes for a long ten-count, blew out her breath in a deep sigh. "I forgot, Hal," she said, aiming for contrite but not quite hitting it. "I mean, I'm not used to being a goddamn industry.

So what if I go out?"

She looked at the other members of the band for support but none was forthcoming. She was meal ticket number one for the moment and everybody seemed to want to keep a close eye on her.

Hal said, "I know the thing next door's not your kind of scene, but MGA went to a whole lot of trouble and expense to arrange it."

"They can afford it," Dee said. "Don't ask me to bleed for them."

Mimi, the blonde groupie, said, "Well, Freddie was really worried about you, Dee, you know. He knocked and knocked, and you did say you had a splitting headache and were going straight to bed."

Dee glanced sharply at the gnome. "You got a key to my room, Hal? I mean, I am a grown-up. There are times when I don't want people busting into my room."

Mimi kept yapping. "Well, you didn't have the Do Not Disturb sign on your door. And we checked Ronny's room — "

"Ron and I are not an exclusive item," Dee said evenly.

"Yeah, well, that's good," Mimi said, with a big smile that didn't reach her eyes. " 'Cause he was having a little party of his own."

"Shut up," Freddie said.

The gnome shrugged. "Just let me know

if you feel the urge to travel after midnight, okay?"

"Carlotta," Dee said after a brief pause, "this is my road manager, Hal Grady. Thinks he's my baby-sitter too. Just let me be, everybody. Okay?"

The dark woman lit a cigarette and nodded in my direction. "So who is she?"

"Bren, this is an old buddy of mine lives in Cambridge. Carlotta, meet Brenda."

We shook hands and Brenda gave me a steady once-over. "You really a cop?" she said.

"No."

"But something like a cop, right?"

"Right," I admitted.

Freddie piped up, "Dee, we really need to fix that A flat major stuff. And this would be a great time. I can really feel it, you know." He smacked the cocktail table like it was a conga drum. "Let me get my trap-set. Hal, you think the people next door would like to hear it?"

"Freddie," Dee said sternly. "Out. And take your girlie with you, okay?"

Mimi, blouse over her arm, made a rush at Dee and gave her an unwanted, enthusiastic hug. She even grabbed my hands in her excitement, and I got a tiny taste of stardom by association.

"Weird Bren gonna get her boy-toy out too?" Freddie asked with a nasty grin.

Brenda patted her companion on his skinny arm, and gave Freddie a look that should have scorched him. The wispy boy on her arm just smiled.

"See you, Dee," the bass player said coolly. "We need to talk, I think. Real soon."

"About the A flat major break?"

"Nah. Freddie's just being stupid about the changes. The stuff works fine. You sure you're okay?"

"Okay," Dee said.

Brenda and her boyfriend exited through the connecting door, heading to the MGA-sponsored bash. Dee gave the drummer the eye until he and his blonde huffed their way out.

The others filed out with no words, just nods. I wasn't sure if Dee even knew them, but Hal, the road manager, did. He asked the sandy-haired guy who'd been sitting on the couch to stay for a second.

"Hal, how'd you get in here?" Dee asked. "Or were those guys in before you?"

"Freddie came by when you didn't answer his knock. I worry too much. I mean, you know, I thought you might be sick or something. I got a spare key at the desk."

"How?"

"Asked for it."

"Tight security," I commented.

Dee said, "Look, Hal. I don't want you thinking I'm passed out any time I don't answer my damn door. I'm not drinking like that anymore."

The road manager studied his running shoes. "It would make a lot of guys happy if you'd come next door for maybe five minutes, ten at the most, shake a few hands."

"Shit," Dee said.

Hal took that for a yes. "Jody," he said to the sandy-haired man. "Get Travis and Marshall and a couple of the other veeps and head them over to the front door. If I walk her through the room, she'll never get out."

Dee gave the sandy-haired man a once-over as he left. Late twenties, early thirties. Thin. Good muscles.

"He work for you?" she asked Hal.

"He works for you," Hal corrected.

"Yeah, well, like I said, I'm a goddamn industry. I oughta get to know my employees better, huh?"

She turned to me. "Come on, Carlotta. Come with me. You ought to see this thing." Then she added under her breath, "And see if you can grab us something to eat. I'm starving to death."

CHAPTER FIVE

Three steps inside the double doors, Dee half screamed in my ear, "Just like old times, huh?"

"Whoo-eee," I hollered in amazed response, "wish I'd worn my formal."

First off, there were the gilt-and-crystal chandeliers. Then there was the wallpaper, painted scenes of pre-Marie Antoinette France, with lots of fluffy sheep tended by buxom shepherdesses falling out of low-cut dresses. Mylar balloons, each inscribed with Dee's *Change Up* album logo, covered the ceiling, trailing gold ribbon tails. The band must have taken a break; the music was DJ-driven rock, three times as loud as a jackhammer. Guests had to shout to be heard.

Then there was the central fountain, which, I swear to God, dispensed champagne. Not that we had to race over and lap it up. A waiter materialized with a silver tray, and Dee and I had glasses in our hands before I could sort out a single face in the crowd.

I turned to say something to Dee, but she was surrounded, engulfed. I shrugged. This mob seemed less threatening than the one in the park.

Waiters kept zooming by with little bits of this and that, and I seized on the strategy of grabbing two of everything, wrapping the doings in cocktail napkins, and thrusting them unobtrusively into my handbag. Dee, her back against a door, champagne in one hand, and a constant parade of well-wishers squeezing the other, never had a chance to snatch so much as a crabmeat-stuffed mushroom.

I'm not a cocktail-party whiz. I hate affairs where you're supposed to stand around in high heels and look like you're enjoying yourself. I could hear Mimi's stoned giggle off to my left, but she didn't seem like someone I wanted to get to know better. I looked for the bass player, but couldn't spot her in the crush.

I saw faces I recognized from TV: local newscasters, sports heroes, and gossip columnists. A few others looked familiar, but I couldn't place them; I thought they might be musicians, hard to identify without their instruments and microphones.

There were men who gave the impression that they'd stepped out of ads in *GQ*, with perfect women on their arms, ladies who looked like they rented by the hour. Then there were the deliberately funky statement-makers, like Mimi in her well-filled black lace bra, and a woman in a skintight catsuit with silver bangle bracelets at wrist and ankles.

There were even a few rhinestone cowboys. All in all, a pretty good sideshow.

On the pocket-sized dance floor, couples — sometimes trios and singles — were doing everything from dignified foxtrots to moves that looked pornographic standing up.

I dumped my empty champagne glass on a passing tray and was rewarded with a full one and a hundred-watt smile from a waiter who looked like he was auditioning for a toothpaste commercial. The smile was wasted on me, but it made me realize the kind of music industry power that must be in the room.

I found myself humming that Joni Mitchell song about "Stoking the starmaker machin'ry behind the popular song." I could have sung it full-volume and nobody would have heard a word.

It looked like Dee would be handshaking forever. I was checking around for a place to sit when I saw a long linen-covered table filled with goodies of every variety, tiny china plates, dainty silver forks. The plates seemed like a better way to stock up for Dee, so I shoved through the crowd and tried to see how many shrimps I could fit in a six-inch circle.

"Nice party, huh?"

Busily spearing shrimp with toothpicks, I

didn't realize the tall man in the tuxedo was speaking to me.

"Okay," I yelled. He seemed vaguely familiar. Big. Beefy. I never watch football or wrestling; if he was a celeb from either field, I wouldn't have seen him play, but I might have caught a news photo if he got injured or caught doing dope.

"There's no place to sit," he observed. Something about the matter-of-fact way he continued the conversation made me wonder if he knew me. I gave him the once-over as subtly as possible. There was a time in my life when I dated a lot of guys, did a bit of indiscriminate one-night-standing, to tell the truth.

"Yeah," I said, agreeing with his comment about the lack of chairs so he wouldn't think I was being deliberately rude. I'd already filled one plate to overflowing. I quickly drank the rest of the champagne, set the glass down, and started loading a second plate. The huddle surrounding Dee was moving back toward the door. I thought she might be attempting an escape.

"You with somebody?" the guy said.

"Huh?"

"You here with somebody? I don't want any guy thinking I'm trying to cut in, you know?"

"I'm a friend of the bride," I said.

He smiled. "I know the groom. We were altar boys together. I'm Mickey, remember?"

Next to me, an angry man in torn jeans and a yellowed T-shirt screamed, "Honey, don't talk to me about royalties. Royalties, hah!"

"Well," a plump black-clad woman responded, "at least you're getting your mechanicals."

Huh? I thought. "Mechanicals" and a guy I couldn't remember. Great party so far.

A woman in tight black slacks, a fuchsia shirt, and batgirl makeup shrieked, "Oh, God, I love it!" in my right ear.

I turned to face her, rarely having heard anyone wax so enthusiastic over shrimp. She was leaning close to a skinny man with a seamed face, a bald pate, and a fringe of long hair. He looked like a member of some group I'd liked a long time ago. He seemed to be singing into her ear.

"You know who that is?" the football player hollered at me.

"Can't say I do."

"Used to be with the Uncle Wigglies. Jimmy Ranger. A regular top-ten hit machine. Produced this album for Willis."

We went on shouting idle party-chatter. I kept hoping he'd mention where we'd met before. If he was hitting on me, he was pretty low-key about it.

"So how's Sam?" he said during a lull in the pounding music.

I only know one Sam: Sam Gianelli, my part-time employer and sometime lover. So I placed the guy then. And I wondered what a man I'd last seen at a Gianelli family funeral — the kind of funeral where the FBI records all the license plate numbers — was doing at a bash in honor of Dee Willis.

CHAPTER SIX

Dee was impressed with my food haul, especially when I kept yanking items out of my bag to add to the two brimming plates.

I was impressed all over again by the size of the room.

"Want to see the bedroom?" Dee asked. "And the bath? Whirlpool, steam, Jacuzzi, whole hog. All attached. One huge suite. Come on. Might as well take a peek. I got to check to see if anybody sneaked in. Two weeks ago, I found some jerk from one of those supermarket sleaze tabloids trying to plant a microphone under my bed."

"If he'd known you better, he could have just planted it in the hall," I said. "Or in an elevator."

Dee drew herself up, all prim and demure. "I have changed," she said in her most exaggerated Southern drawl. "I am the silent type. And I only do it in bed. Most of the time, anyway."

The tour was worth the price of admission. In the huge bedroom, a king-size bed sat on a platform like a throne on a dais. Its canopy was swagged in gold brocade. So were the tall windows that stared out over Boston Common. A bowl of fruit on an end table looked like it was posing for a still life.

We carried the fruit bowl into the living room in the interest of nutritional balance. A gift card from MGA/America was tucked between an orange and a pomegranate. Dee excused herself to go to the bathroom. Since I was nosing around anyway, I checked the flower arrangement: compliments of the management.

I stay in hotels where the management is stingy about plastic drinking cups.

Dee rejoined me, grabbing the plateful of shrimp.

"Cocktail sauce?" she said hopefully.

"Under there somewhere."

"Great."

I was halfway through a tiny spinach pie wrapped in filo dough. "Your arm okay?" I asked.

She chewed, ignored my question, and said, "Bet I could still find your aunt Bea's old house. Bet I could find it in the dark."

"It's mine now."

"I heard she died." Dee kicked off her shoes, sat on the sofa opposite me, one leg tucked up behind her. Her toenails were painted powder pink. "I kinda miss old Bea."

"C'mon, Dee," I said.

"No," she went on, chatting too brightly, too fast, "honestly, I do. I miss everybody. I miss all the old times. I miss people I hated. Remember Alice? Remember *Denny?* I mean, if that little twerp walked in here right now, I'd roll over like an ol' puppy dog and lick his face — except, you know, honey, I think that's the one part Denny never wanted me to lick."

She stuck her tongue out, and I grinned. Ten years ago — pre-Cal — I might have rolled over and licked her face too.

"You know what time it is?" I inquired in mock despair.

"Late, huh? I know. I'm dead too. We were rehearsing before the party. Last-minute stuff. I'm here to kick off this concert tour. Jimmy, that's Jimmy Ranger, my producer on this last album and, pray God, the next, flew in special to check out the mix, and I'm higher than a kite, I know it. Not drugs, Carlotta. Not any of that shit. Not anymore. Just, you know, adrenaline." She leaned forward suddenly, snapped her fingers a couple of inches from my face. "It came to me, just like that, when I saw you in the cab. You're the one."

"Maybe," I said warily. "Maybe not."

"You never give me a straight yes or no."

"You're always so pushy," I said at the same time. We both glared at each other, and I felt like I ought to be sitting on the floor of her old Mass. Ave. apartment, barefoot, with a guitar in my hands, inhaling a roomful of dope.

It was marijuana back then; coke cost too much.

I never smoked the stuff, what with my dad a cop, and me going for the police academy. I stuck to my cigarettes, courting lung cancer. At Dee's you didn't have to smoke dope to get high. All you had to do was breathe.

"You know many people at the party?" I asked.

"The band. A few of the roadies and techies. Far as MGA/America goes, my people meet with their people. I probably got introduced to about a thousand guys tonight, but I wouldn't know 'em tomorrow. My hand feels like hamburger. That's how I got out of there. Told Hal if I shook one more hand, I wouldn't be able to pick a note."

"The name 'Mickey' or 'Big Mickey' mean anything to you?" I couldn't remember the last name of the man who'd asked about Sam Gianelli. Or maybe I'd never known it.

"Mickey Mouse. I remember him. Look, let's get down to business." She licked cocktail sauce off a fingertip, then tried folding her hands in her lap. She seemed restless; it looked more like her left hand was grabbing the right

60

to keep it still. "Could you find Davey for me?"

"Davey?"

"Davey Dunrobie."

I hadn't thought about Dunrobie twice in ten years. "Hell," I said impulsively, "I'd love to find him, see if he still looks that good."

"I knew you'd do it."

"Whoa, Dee. This is what I do for a living."

"I'm gonna pay," she protested, hand to her heart. "I'll pay you for this; it's not like a favor or anything."

"When was the last time you saw him?" I asked.

My question seemed to catch her off balance. "Well, uh, I . . . Do I need to tell you stuff like that?"

"Only if you want me to work for you." I reached out and grabbed a shrimp, ice-cold, firm and sweet, tail attached. I dipped it in red sauce, dribbling on my white shirt. "You can hire somebody else."

"But you know him, Carlotta. Nobody else knows Dunrobie, knows what he looks like even."

"I admit I've got the inside track. But you have to give me someplace to start."

"Well, shit," she said. "You knew him."

"Nice seeing you, Dee."

"Sit down, Carlotta, it's just . . . Damn.

It's hard to talk about. Davey was my first partner."

"There was Lorraine," I said quietly. "The group. You remember: me on rhythm guitar, Cal on bass, Lorraine sharing the vocals with you and shaking the tambourine — "

"Yeah." She cut my memories short. "But he was my first, you know, professional partner. Shit, I must have gray hair."

"Tina Turner's older than you," I said. "Relax."

"Mick Jagger's older than me," she said.

"You look great," I said. "And you know it. So cut the crap. Were you looking for Dunrobie tonight? In junior-grade needle park?"

She couldn't find another way to stall, so she leaned forward, and spoke softly, as if people were listening on all sides.

"Let me start from the top," she said. "You know, after we — uh, after the group split up, I went and formed the band and all. And Dunrobie, well, it's sad what happened to him. I mean, you ever hear a sweeter, finer voice than Dunrobie's? You ever hear a better guitar picker?"

I had, but not many, and she didn't seem to want answers to her questions.

"Dunrobie had more fans than me. He had women flinging themselves all over him.

You thought one of the two of us was gonna make it, which would it be? Dunrobie, right? Davey every time."

Again I kept still. I'd have picked Dee ten times out of ten. She always had that burning, hungry quality. Dunrobie had seemed overwhelmed by even minor successes. Cal had once described Davey as a 3 B man, the kind of musician who's good enough to play any town and come out of it with the all-important beer, burger, and blow-job.

Dee was saying, "It's like this: Dunrobie started to drink. Not like the rest of us. I mean, he drank like he did it for a living. And after he finished drinking, he downed every kind of recreational chemical he could beg or buy, and pretty soon he couldn't get work as a ditchdigger, much less a guitar player."

"I didn't know," I said.

"Maybe five years ago, I came into town, not playing anyplace, just trying to line up some gigs, and I ran into Davey. He was this bum, this shambling old man in a park, maybe a mile from the public library. Better than most. I mean, he wasn't mumbling to himself or anything, but he was staring at the grass like there wasn't anything in the world gonna interest him ever again. Dunrobie always had that little thing wrong with the way he walked — "

"The hockey injury."

"Wasn't it football?" Dee said. "Shit, he probably fell down a flight of stairs and told everybody some kind of romantic crap. Anyway, the limp clinched it. I walked right up to him and put my hand on his shoulder, and he jumped like I was gonna steal his last dime. He *smelled,* Carlotta. He stank. I bought him a cup of coffee, and you should have seen the faces in that café when I came in with him. Honest, the looks on their faces. And I tried to make him eat a meal, you know. I wanted to do something, and finally I talked him into letting me give him some rent money. You know, you get to a point where two hundred bucks, what's it gonna do for you? You buy a blouse for it, right? Get your hair streaked. And here I could give Dunrobie a couple hundred, and he could make the security deposit on a place to live, just a room, you know, but it was all he'd take, and he swore it was just a loan and he'd pay me back and all that."

Dee was staring at the floor like she was embarrassed at being caught in a good deed.

"Well," she continued when I didn't say anything, "I asked him to keep in touch, but I never found out the name of the street he was planning to live on. He didn't have a phone. Then maybe a year later, four years ago, he started calling, oh, maybe twice a year, and honey, he had the worst luck. God, everything happened to Dunrobie. He got kicked out of his room. He lost his shoe-clerk job because his boss hit on him. His landlord wanted him to go to work in his snow-shoveling business and quit playing that guitar all night. His dog died. He was always phoning me with some sorry tale and I was always sending him a money order care of somebody or other, usually a woman, and that was fine. I mean, I made it clear to him, I hope to hell I did, that I didn't want him living on the streets while I was putting money into a bank account for my old age. You might die young, I always say."

"I wish I'd known about Dunrobie."

"Well, now you do, and you can find him for me. That's what I was trying to do tonight, only it seems like it was a rotten idea. I haven't heard from him in over a year, fourteen months. I mean, maybe he's sobered up, and doing fine. I don't want the money back, even if he's living in a palace. I'm worried about him."

"That's all?" I said.

"What do you mean all?" she asked. "Isn't that enough?"

"Well," I said, "let me tell you. A missing persons search is either easy or it's hard. Either you find something right away, like his name and number in the phone book, or you can't find anything at all. You should have filled out a report while we were at the police station."

"Carlotta, the drugs he did, I'm not going to point some cop in his direction. If he's still hooked, that's all he'd need."

"Okay," I said, "I see your point. What I'm saying is that the cost varies because missing persons stuff is dicey. I take a fee up front and I charge for expenses, and then I charge for results. If I get results, it costs."

"Carlotta, I'm playing the Berklee Performance Center Saturday night. I mean, it's not a giant stadium, not like some of the places on this tour, but it means a whole lot to me. The acoustics are incredible. Jimmy Ranger's here, recording some live cuts for a new album. Believe me, I can afford your rates, and I want Dunrobie there. I need to look in the audience Saturday night and see certain faces. I need Dunrobie."

"This Saturday?" I said skeptically. It was only four days off, but unless he was hiding, I was almost sure I'd be able to locate him by then. Still, magicians have to make a few fancy passes before they pull rabbits out of their hats. Otherwise nobody applauds.

"Carlotta, see what you can do."

"Sometimes I have to mail requests for information. Saturday's not enough time to do a state-by-state motor vehicle check."

"But you could do local stuff."

I shrugged. "If he's local, I can get him. If he's local and he drives, I can get him in twenty minutes. Hotel have stationery?"

She pointed me toward a desk and I opened the top drawer and found a sheet with gold lettering at the top. A slim white pen sat next to a white phone. I used it to print David Dunrobie's name at the top of the page. Then I sat in the desk chair and started asking Dee all the questions, beginning with Dunrobie's middle name.

"How the hell should I know?" she said. "You still have that rotten National guitar?"

"Last known address? You still have that crummy Dobro?"

"I guess that would be the dump on Mass. Ave., when he was living with me. Eight-sixty-five, I think."

"His name on the lease?"

"No."

We amazed ourselves with our ignorance. We didn't know who Dunrobie's parents were, whether he had any sisters or brothers. We sure didn't know his social security number.

"Shit, Carlotta," Dee said finally. "Why don't you ask the right questions? I can tell you he was one fine lay."

I grinned, and took the last shrimp. "I didn't have to ask, Dee."

"You too?" she crowed. "Jeez, I didn't know that. Look, it's been a hell of a long day, and I'm starting to crash. Find Dunrobie for me. I always do a good show Saturday night. Find him before then."

I said, "Four hundred will buy you a day. I can hit all the easy places in a day. Ten to one, I'll find him."

She looked around the room like she was searching for something. "Hey, damn," she said when she realized her handbag was gone, "can I pay you later?"

"Company policy," I said. "I don't work till I get paid."

"Will a check be okay?"

I hesitated.

"Anytime you want to sell that rotten National guitar, you call me," she said. "And let me give you some comps for the concert. Six enough?"

"From old friends, I take checks," I said.

"Okay!" she said, elated, slapping her hands together with a single loud report.

"I don't suppose you want to tell me why you really want to find Dunrobie," I said.

"Huh?"

"You're suddenly in such a rush, after five

years, that you run out of a party held in your honor — "

"I hate big parties. And I want him at that concert Saturday."

"Sure," I said. "Berklee Performance Center's a big place. You won't exactly be able to stare into his eyes for inspiration."

She kept her head down while she wrote the check, and she didn't say another word.

CHAPTER SEVEN

I deposited the check in the BayBank machine near the Central Square Y after playing my regular volleyball match. I didn't want to wait till the bank opened.

By nine, I was glued to my desk telephone, calling sources cultivated through the years, many of whom I met when I was a cop. A clerk at the Registry of Motor Vehicles, the regular recipient of a Christmas bottle of Johnnie Walker Red, disappointed me. He couldn't find any cars registered in Dunrobie's name. I took a sip of coffee laced with sugar and cream, and sighed. I'd considered the Registry my best bet.

I punched the next number, gossiped for a few minutes with an old acquaintance who works at the CORI unit of the Office for Children. Patsy Alvarez prefers Swiss chocolates to whiskey for Christmas. I learned that Dunrobie had absolutely no arrest record, not even a "driving while intoxicated," which fit right in with his having no driver's license.

I'd had visions of a recent "drunk and disorderly" at least. I'd been hoping to track him quickly; impress hell out of Dee, I admitted to myself.

Next phone call: The U.Mass. Alumni Office refused, like all university alumni offices, to give out an address, but I managed to wheedle the fact that they had none to withhold in Dunrobie's case. He hadn't graduated.

Most of the people in our crowd were U.Mass. kids, but Dee had gone to Berklee for a time, so I dialed the Berklee School of Music and spent a lot of time on hold, listening to a decent FM classical station. Dunrobie had not attended Berklee.

Ditto the New England Conservatory of Music.

Under "Labor Unions" in the Yellow Pages, I found the American Guild of Musical Artists. They had no Dunrobie as a member. I hesitated for a long minute, then hung up.

I finished the coffee. Seemed like Davey had dropped far out of sight. No driver's license, no union card. I wondered if Dee had been serious about him trying construction work. I called two carpenter union locals. No Dunrobies.

I changed out of my sweats into khaki pants, a print shirt, and a navy linen blazer, an outfit that makes me look trustworthy and professional. Shoulder bag swinging, I hit the Bureau of Vital Statistics at the State House and struck out on Davey's birth certificate, which would have contained all sorts of useful goodies, like his mom's maiden name, and his date of birth. Dee and I had agreed that he was older than the rest of us, but we weren't sure if it was two years or four years or what.

I walked from the State House to the Public Library, wishing I'd chosen more comfortable shoes, soothed by the thought that the MBTA would be even more unbearably hot than the overland route. You'd think the subways, being underground, would stay cool, but by August they've soaked up all the city heat and stink. Some of the cars are air-conditioned, granted, but you can never count on boarding one. I slowed when I came to Copley Square Park and stared at the homeless men seated like statues on the benches. Would I recognize Davey Dunrobie with ten hard years added, and maybe a beard and a layer of grime?

At the library, I checked telephone directories for the last twelve years, the cross-directories as well. There were no Dunrobies at all, which I found discouraging. I hadn't expected him to be listed, but I'd had hopes of finding a brother or a cousin.

I couldn't help myself; I looked it up. In the 1979 book: Therieux, Calvin and Carlotta. Ma Bell had gotten it wrong as usual; I'd never taken his last name. They'd printed the address correctly, half a low-rent duplex in Cambridgeport.

There was no current listing for Cal.

I breathed a sigh of relief. He and Dunrobie used to be buddies. If I'd found a listing for Cal, I'd have felt honor-bound to call, see if he knew where I might find Davey. I wondered if I'd have disguised my voice.

I asked two friendly librarians if they remembered a guy who looked like Dunrobie gone to seed, especially one who listened to a lot of music. For the first time, I thought about my junk drawer; it would have been useful to flash a photo of Dunrobie, no matter how out-of-date.

"We have a hundred guys like that," the librarians agreed, which was no help to me. "Especially in winter. Who wouldn't rather listen to music in a heated building than sit and shiver in the cold?"

I visited the Pine Street Inn, a shelter for the homeless, and drew a lot of blank stares. I stuffed a few bills in the donation box, and hoped none of my old friends was sleeping on a charity cot. I dropped in on the Salvation Army. I didn't even try Alcoholics Anonymous. They're just that: anonymous.

The Copley Square/South End area and Dee's old place in Cambridge were the only locales I had for Dunrobie. I visited the appropriate post offices, urged harried clerks to check the records of forwarding addresses, the removal books — but nothing doing.

I saved the Central Square Post Office for last because it was closest to home. I thought about strolling the neighborhood, bumping doors, asking folks if they knew a guy who drank and played the guitar. Without a photo, it rated right up there with Dee handing out ten-spots in a South End park.

So I walked home, opened my junk drawer, and like Pandora, let the demons fly.

CHAPTER EIGHT

When my aunt Bea died, she left twenty-two stout cardboard boxes tied with twine in the crawl space off the attic. "Mementos," she called them. I've never opened them; I try not to think about them.

I'm not big on keepsakes, nor am I much of a collector. Searching crime scenes as a cop cured me of that. I used to find myself feeling doubly sorry for victims; not only had they been raped, robbed, or killed — now they had a troop of strangers snooping through their stained underwear.

After my first scene-of-the-crime search I'd raced home and tossed out bagfuls of potential embarrassments, from mail-order creams guaranteed to increase your breast size in thirty-days-or-your-money-back to gushy poetry written by my ninth-grade sweetheart.

I stared uneasily at the bedside table, at the deep bottom drawer on the right-hand side of the bed, farthest from the doorway, repository of, among other odds and ends, my wedding photos.

I don't own a camera. Roz, my inadequate housecleaner, resident post-punk artist, and sometime assistant, handles my work-related photographic needs for a fee. I dislike taking photos, but people tend to give them to you, and it somehow seems wrong to discard those beaming frozen faces. I stick them in my junk drawer.

Paolina's school photos are the exception. She's my little sister from the Big Sisters Organization, and I keep her current photo in a silver frame on the living room mantel.

Paolina and I are temporarily estranged. Her mother won't let me see her, thanks to complications left over from a case of mine. I admit that I may have screwed up — and Paolina's life was endangered. But what frosts me is that it's not the danger that's got Paolina's mother in a snit. It's the fact that Paolina learned a few new items about herself, things Mama had been trying to hide.

I've got a social worker trying to reunite us, and I write to Paolina three times a week. I just hope that Marta, her mother, passes along the letters. She won't even let me talk to Paolina on the phone, and the damned social worker keeps saying to give it time, give it time.

I sat cross-legged on the floor, yanked open the drawer, and coughed at the lingering smell of old dusting powder — something cheap I'd thought sexy one summer in my teens. Emerald something. It conjured up a greasy-haired boy named Doug I'd dated twice in high school. A forbidden midnight boat ride.

It's been years since I was a cop, and I guess my fear of scene-of-the-crime searches is starting to fade. Amazing, the idiotic items I've stuck in that drawer. Free samples — everything from face cream to breakfast cereal. Shoulder pads ripped out of jackets that made me look like a defensive lineman. Half-empty cans of birth-control foam. A collection of very personal birthday cards from Sam Gianelli.

Just the stuff I'd love to have cops rooting through. I went downstairs and got an empty grocery sack. I tossed the breakfast cereal samples first, wondering why I hadn't kept them in the kitchen, hoping they hadn't attracted cockroaches. Underneath a tiny box of Raisin Nut Bran, I discovered an even tinier pair of hot-pink bikini panties. Why on earth? Oh, yeah, the elastic had stretched when I'd ignored the wash-by-hand warning. Had I really meant to replace the elastic? I tossed them in the sack. I'm as good a seamstress as Roz is a housecleaner.

I found the wedding photos lodged under a three-year-old issue of *Mother Jones*. They're collected in a slim white album. The bride in the pictures smiled, but I really couldn't connect her blurred face with mine. I made myself search carefully, but the photographer, my mother's half-wit cousin Lou from Kansas City, trying out his third profession in as many months, had blown every possibly useful close-up of the wedding party.

Davey had been a last-minute addition to that select group, pressed into duty as best man in lieu of Cal's no-show alcoholic father.

Since I'd been married in my hometown, Detroit, not many of my Boston friends had attended. I flipped another page. In one surprisingly clear group shot, a sweep of the entire room, Davey Dunrobie was a flyspeck in a corner, nothing you could show around.

All the same, I put the photograph aside. Maybe Roz would know some magical way to enlarge it.

Lorraine's photo must have been stuck in the back of the album. It fluttered to the ground and I stared at it, transfixed by her innocent smile.

"After the first death there is no other," Dylan Thomas says in one of the few lines of verse I remember without trying. Lorraine was my first. A friend who killed herself at twenty-two.

I picked the print up carefully, held it so

the light didn't glare. She hadn't been pretty, although she might have grown handsome with the years she hadn't used. What she looked mainly, I thought, was young. Unformed, unlined, unshaped.

It must have been snapped at a picnic. I could see a card table off to one side, paper tablecloth anchored with baskets of potato chips, bottles of Coke and beer. Someone's blue-jeaned behind was visible off to the left. I couldn't tell if it belonged to a man or a woman.

There was a time when I believed I'd mourn Lorraine every day of my life. But in fact I hadn't thought about her for months, years. Maybe a brief moment on the anniversary of her death, near Halloween with the chill of fall.

I asked myself the old question, why? At the memorial service, Lorraine's mother had confided that her daughter had been seeing a shrink — hardly the commonplace occurrence of today. By the time I saw Lorraine's apartment, her parents had stripped it bare. All her notebooks, all her papers, had been crated and shipped to Norfolk, Virginia. Her mother had given me a Jesse Colin Young album and Lorraine's mandolin as keepsakes. A line from a song on the album came unbidden to my mind.

"Four in the mornin'
and the water is pourin' down."

I must have played that cut a hundred times. Then I stuck the record somewhere up in the attic, along with the mandolin and Aunt Bea's untouched boxes.

The first question, why?, was automatically followed by the next, how could I not have known? How could I have partied and sung and joked with Lorraine, and never sensed her sadness and despair? How could I drink a routine cup of coffee with a friend on Friday and learn of her suicide Saturday night?

Oh, Lorraine. I felt a flash of anger, followed by immediate guilt. I put her picture on my bed, then hurriedly stuck it back in the album. I knew I could stare at it forever and provoke nothing more than a bad case of the three A.M. what-ifs.

I stuck my hand way in the back of the drawer, searching for my stack of little black books.

I've never been tempted to keep a diary, but I do maintain a date book, a business thing, mileage and parking fees, where I've been when. Lunch dates and birthday reminders. I hang on to them more for tax purposes than sentiment.

Had I kept my black books back then? They

had to date from my first charge card, an account at the Harvard Coop that made me feel very adult and full of myself at the time. The Coop, pronounced as in "chicken coop" even though it's a contraction of co-operative, sends out an academic year calendar to all members, a tiny thing, less than three by five, black with thinly ruled pages. A new one arrives like clockwork in July, and I toss the old one in the drawer.

I thumbed through the pile to find the right year. 1977–78 would be best.

I found the black books for '82–'83, '78–'79, '81–'82, stacked them in chronological order. Seventy-eight was as far back as they seemed to run. The first pages of each book had tables of weights and measures, lists of holidays. Then there were a few blank pages for phone numbers and addresses. I checked to see if I had entered either for Dunrobie.

I found Dee's name heavily crossed out at 555-8765, a Cambridge number, probably the Mass. Ave. apartment. I checked through the rest of the phone numbers, most of them hurriedly scrawled, with only a first name to tag them. Gary at a 734 exchange. Had I known a Gary? A Ken? Alice? That must have been Alice Jackson. Hadn't she married, and what the hell had she changed her name to? She might remember Dunrobie.

I tried the number written next to Alice. The man who answered was querulous, elderly, and quite certain no Alice was in any way connected with his phone number. He'd had it the past five years, ever since he moved up from Memphis, Tennessee, and nobody ever called much, and certainly not for any Alice. His first wife was named Mary Alice, and he sure would have remembered.

I went doggedly through the book and came up with another possibility: Angela, a blonde with pale lashes, a long nose. I punched the number and got a male voice on an answering machine. I have an answering machine myself, but I hate talking to them. I hung up.

I had phone numbers for a Jeff and a Susan, as if the people I'd met in my teens and twenties had only first names. As if I'd thought I'd always remember who they were. Asking about people's backgrounds seemed so intrusive then. If somebody had a distinctive accent, you might ask where they were from, but that was it. Maybe I shied away from that kind of talk because I never wanted to admit my father was a cop. But the other kids were the same. No last names required.

Nobody at Jeff's number answered.

I found two phone numbers scrawled on the last page. I figured one of them had to be Cal's. With no names attached, they had to be numbers I called often, or numbers I never planned to call again. I shrugged and tried the first. Three beeps from NYNEX, and a recorded "This number has been disconnected. Please check your listing and dial again."

The second number picked up after six rings with a recorded message in a male voice. "Hi. You've reached 555-4647. Tell me what you think I ought to know."

It was a fine deep voice, relaxed and easy. If I'd heard it before I would have remembered it.

I hung up, then redialed the two recorded-message phones, leaving the bare minimum: my name, phone number, and a request to call as soon as possible on an urgent matter. Curiosity wins out more often than not.

I checked through the rest of the books and got nothing but wrong numbers and dead ends.

Reluctantly, I phoned Dee at the hotel.

I could tell there were visitors in her room by the cautious way she spoke and the voices in the background.

"You do it?" she asked.

"I can tell you where he isn't," I said. "Sorry."

"I need to see you," she said with forced cheerfulness. "We're at the Performance Center tonight, rehearsal, maybe lay down a few tracks for the album. Start at seven and work right through. Drop by?"

I hesitated.

"Come on," she urged. "Maybe I'll let you play Miss Gibson."

Any blues picker worth a bottleneck slide would crawl to the corner of Mass. Ave. and Boylston Street for a chance to play the Reverend Gary Davis's old guitar.

CHAPTER NINE

I was standing near the theater, flipping a mental coin over front- versus backdoor etiquette, when Mimi, the curly-haired blonde, sailed around the corner, and almost mowed me down.

I fell into step beside her. "Remember me? Dee's friend."

"Oh, sure," she replied, smiling for all she was worth. She was swinging hand in hand with a young man who was wearing one gold hoop earring that made him look like a pirate. She wore tights and a tank top in tiger stripes, a matching headband, and black lace-up boots. Roz, my personal arbiter of fashion taste, would have found her a bit passé.

She blitzed through the front door and I followed; no doubt she was with a band hanger-on — not drummer Freddie tonight, but somebody who at least knew somebody semi-famous.

I had always figured rehearsals for major-league concerts would be pretty closed affairs. If you're charging $27.50 a seat, you don't want to give it away in advance. But nobody challenged me as I marched across the lobby in Mimi's perfumed wake.

She and the boy with the hoop earring disappeared through swinging aisle-doors. I followed. Inside the auditorium a humming screech rose and fell. Lights flickered. A disembodied voice echoed over a loudspeaker, calling for Pre-set Twelve, and telling Holly, for chrissake, to check the left 7 amp.

When I played with Dee, in that short-lived unmourned group, Cambridge Common, we were acoustic. Tuning our instruments was all the foreplay we needed.

A small army of electricians and stagehands scrambled on and off the stage. A scrawny boy-girl in unisex jeans and shirt carefully set Dee's Dobro, along with a twelve-string of more recent vintage, and a bright blue Stratocaster, on metal stands. A boy in jeans crawled along the floor checking cable connections and muttering into a headset.

Dee was an industry, all right.

On either side of the tall proscenium arch loomed stacks of boxy amplifiers: Fenders, Vox AC-30s, Bandmasters. Cables crisscrossed the floor. The stage was divided by platforms and risers. Freddie, the drummer; a keyboard man; and Brenda, the bass player, stood three steps above Dee and her lead guitar.

Ron. The one with whom Dee was less than

exclusively involved. I wondered if Dee had ever been exclusively involved with anyone.

Dee was chatting with the drummer, oblivious to the commotion. Freddie tapped out a syncopated rhythm, using a muffled stick and a brush on an impressive trap-set — silvery snares, sides, and tom-toms, all banded in brass — a pair of hi-hat cymbals, two regulars, and a rack of chimes and bells.

Across stage, Brenda hit a few deep notes on her Fender bass and frowned at their wavering echo. She shouted something into the wings. Somebody fiddled with an amp. The hum stopped abruptly.

Dee strolled downstage, leaned over, and spoke into a microphone. "We okay out there?" she said, her voice low and husky. "Jimmy, how's the pick-up?"

"Okay."

"Who's riding gain?"

"Me, honey," came a different voice. "I got you loud and clear, and you're gorgeous."

I slid into an aisle seat way down front.

Dee shouldered her six-string, plugged in the pick-up, crossed to Brenda. They tried a chord together. Dee fingered a few notes, bent some of them. She was wearing a slide on the little finger of her left hand. Her guitar strap looked like snakeskin, with a big gold buckle.

The amplified voice said, "Okay, boys and girls, this is a take," and all the stagehands vanished. Dee moved center stage, still talking over her shoulder to the bass player. She tapped her vocal mike with a fingernail, adjusted her instrument mike, tapped her toe hard eight times in the sudden hush, and music happened.

The keyboard player started it, but the sound could have been a keening horn. Brenda picked it up on bass. The drummer came in rocking. The lead guitar hit the opening riff. It had changed a lot, but I recognized it, the song Dee had once called her anthem: "For Tonight."

The vocal entered with a tough-gal sexy edge.

> "Don't need anybody to cry out my name,
>   Don't need anybody to care.
> Don't need anybody to tug at my skirt,
>   Don't need anybody to share.
>
> For tonight, for a while, I want you.
> For tonight, for a while, I want you."

It was a standard rocker, heavily blues-influenced, and fleshed out with a lot of fancy guitar. Dee had written it at a time when most of the hits were sentimental love songs. Recorded by more popular singers, it had kept her afloat through lean years.

She was starting the second verse when the amplified voice interrupted. "Cut there, okay? Brenda, we're getting a hell of a lot of reverb."

The drummer crashed a forlorn cymbal, and Dee said, "Oh, come on, Brenda, get with it."

She may have meant to mutter it under her breath, but she forgot about the microphone.

Brenda shot her a look. Somebody in the audience giggled. I suspected good old Mimi.

"Can we pick it up at twenty-four?" Dee asked.

"Start over. I might need a few extra tracks for the live cut."

This time the lighting crew got into the act. They messed around with their colored gels at first, but they quickly got the hang of which-performer-to-highlight-when. Probably had a roadie up in the booth giving cues.

The houselights faded to black.

I stopped concentrating on the technical crap, closed my eyes, and listened. All those quarts of whiskey hadn't dulled Dee's voice. Playing bars for drinks and food seemed to have honed it, stripped away the extra trills and flourishes. Too many cigarettes had put a growl into the lower register, a weary moan into the high notes. Her style hadn't changed;

it was more like she'd grown into it, become the sassy, jaded blueswoman she'd always tried to be.

My shoulder bag bit into my side. I put it on the empty worn velvet seat beside me.

Dee slid into an old Billie Holiday thing, then livened the set with a Delta blues, maybe John Lee Hooker. She was moving with the music, almost dancing, but it didn't seem showy or out of place, didn't even look planned. It was just part of the song, a sexy harmony.

I don't look straitlaced or anything, not with my tumbled red hair. But Dee, well, the word "sensual" springs to mind. Dee, when she plays guitar, looks like she has nothing on her mind but sex. I don't know if she was born that way, lips slightly parted, eyes smoldering, or whether it comes from singing lowdown, dirty blues.

I can practice a song and practice it, and when I get it right — right notes, right tempo, clean fingering — I'm through. I lose interest and move on to the next song. I can pour heart and soul into the effort of learning, but once the song is there, whatever magic has occurred is over and done.

Dee takes the practiced song, and then she starts her magic. She sings her stuff as if she's making it up on the spot, as if she's got something urgent to tell you, and isn't it nice that the band happened along. She sings like she's got a secret, and if you listen long enough, she'll tell it to you — and only you.

My eyes grew accustomed to the dark and I glanced at a guy two rows up on the aisle. He looked like he'd forgotten to breathe.

Dee wore a white tuxedo jacket and white pants. She kept the jacket buttoned, but her apparent lack of a shirt was quite a come-on. The lights made her a rainbow. And she moved and sang and played as though the songs were pouring out of her, as if she'd never have enough time to tell us all the things she needed to say.

While Dee was lit with the dancing spotlights, her group played in shadow unless spotted for a solo. Her lead guitar looked tall and wiry. The drummer hid behind tinted glasses and a scowl. Today his wristbands and headband were neon-green. The keyboard player, a scruffy youngster with a two-day stubble, kept his head thrown back, never staring down for the notes, his eyes closed in ecstasy. Brenda seemed less involved than the rest, more laid-back, as if she alone were clued in to the fact that this was just another rehearsal. Dee didn't seem to be holding anything back.

In the middle of the sixth song, Dee hit

a deliberately dissonant, jarring chord, and backed away from the mike, eyes flashing. "Jimmy," she yelled, "are you listening to this shit or what?"

"Yeah, hon, what do you want?"

"Are you hearing that bass line?"

"I'm hearing it."

"Well?"

"Well, what?"

"Well, it's not what we've been doing, is it? It's not what I want."

Brenda said, "I thought I'd give it a try."

Dee said, "You talk to me first next time."

"I've been trying to talk to you for two damn days, and you're all of a sudden so busy, nobody can freaking find you. I thought you'd like it."

"It stinks, Bren. It sounds like a goddamn dog howling."

"Kind of like a bitch, you mean?" Brenda said with a nasty edge to her voice. I decided to give her the same benefit of the doubt I'd given Dee: maybe she meant to mutter it under her breath, but her microphone picked it up and echoed it clear to the balcony.

"What did you say?" Dee asked.

The amplified voice interrupted her. "Okay, Brenda, can you just do what Dee wants here with the bass?"

"No, Jimmy, I can't. It's too damn boring.

I'm gonna freaking fall asleep."

Dee said, "Well, I can find fifty bass players glad to do it, better than you can anytime."

"Oh, yeah?" Brenda unplugged her instrument, lifted it over her head, and carefully laid it down on the floorboards. Then she gave Dee the finger and walked offstage.

"Bren, get the hell back here," the drummer yelled into his mike. His volume overloaded some circuit and the whole business fed back with a high-pitched hum that made me slap my hands over my ears.

"Jimmy," Dee was saying, "I talked to her about that break a hundred times. It's a blues thing, not a rock thing. I want something easy and bluesy. She's giving me all this hyperactive-note shit."

"Take ten," Jimmy's voice said wearily. The houselights snapped on and the sound technicians and the light technicians and the stagehands swarmed.

Dee shaded her eyes with her hand and surveyed the audience. I waved, and she yelled, "Hi," and motioned me up onstage.

I reached over to the seat next to me to grab my handbag, a reflex move. There was nothing but air on the shabby red cushion. I quickly flipped up the seat, looked underneath, groped around on the sticky floor, and scanned the whole area. My bag was gone.

"You coming, Carlotta?"

"Shit," I mumbled under my breath. "Coming," I shouted out loud. I gave a quick glance around the auditorium: maybe fifty people. A movement at the top of the far aisle caught my eye, just the glimpse of a foot, the flash of a closing door.

"Be right back!" I yelled at Dee, and I took off.

CHAPTER TEN

I sprinted through the double aisle-doors, glanced left and right, saw movement from the direction of the lobby. I skidded left and went after it, just as if I were wearing a uniform.

The gnomelike man I'd met at the impromptu party in Dee's room appeared out of nowhere. I almost careened into him. He yelled something as I ran by.

I could barely see the snatch-artist once I got outside. If he'd slowed his pace, tried to blend in with the street strollers, I'd have given up. But he kept running.

A novice.

He was a young tan kid in gang colors, wearing a watch cap in spite of the heat. Slight build. Five-six. I tried to get the details straight while I ran, but it was dark and I was furious about my handbag. I'm rarely careless with it. I almost never put it down. I even wear the strap crossed over my chest, bandolero-style, the better to frustrate hit-and-run snatchers.

Lulled by Dee's songs, I'd tossed it on a chair and forgotten its existence.

It wasn't the money. It wasn't the credit cards. It was the sheer effrontery, the inconvenience it would cause, and the photo of my mom and dad — together and smiling for once — that kept me running. Not to mention wounded pride.

"Stop!" I shouted at the first corner. The street noises ate the sound. Cars honked.

The thief kept racing up Mass. Ave. toward the Christian Science Center and the Mother Church. I cursed my crummy running shoes — leather soles, not rubber. I was sliding with every sweaty step. By the end of the third block, I realized I was gaining inches, not feet, and I started looking for a cop car, knowing I'd hardly get lucky twice in a row. I could hear running footsteps trailing far behind me.

The kid had too good a head start. He would have gotten away easily if he hadn't stumbled on a curb. He hit pavement next to a broken-down Chevy. He lay winded for a moment, and then started to use the car fender to boost himself back up.

"Drop the bag," I yelled. At the same time my hand clamped onto his wrist. He had the bag in his other hand, but he neatly slid his arm through the strap, made a grab for the back of his pants, and came up with a knife.

It was a folding blade, maybe five inches, and he held it like an extension of his hand.

"You crazy bastard," I said softly.

"Hey, watch it, lady." The warning came from behind me. It snapped me out of my daze, and I let go of the kid's wrist and stood motionless while he backed off, breathing hard. I memorized his narrow, high-cheekboned face, the acne on his nose and chin. I couldn't get the color of his eyes in the dim light, and that pissed me off because I wanted to be a good witness at the trial.

Goddammit, what trial? Who the hell gives a damn about purse snatchers?

The kid turned tail and ran.

Hal, Dee's road manager, appeared at my side. "I saw you shoot out of the lobby like your hair was on fire. What the hell was that all about? You almost knocked me on my ass."

"Forget it," I said to him, passing a hand over my sweaty forehead, trying to bring my breathing and temper under control. "He had a knife."

"I saw that! Jesus, I saw! You don't go up against somebody with a knife! You into that martial arts crap? A lot of good that does against a knife or a gun. I got a daughter myself. She ever chased after a guy with a knife, I'd — Shit, I don't know what I'd do."

I watched the kid disappear across Mass. Ave. into the maze of streets behind Symphony Hall.

Hal said, "So, what happened?"

"Guy stole my purse."

I started marching back toward the Performance Center, walking fast to get the anger and adrenaline out.

"Right in the Center? You want to call a cop?"

"They don't even fill out a form," I said, which is not true. It's just that they don't do a lot more than fill out a form. Purse snatching is one of those crimes that's so commonplace that the cops treat the victims like jerks. Well, what the hell do you expect, lady, carrying a handbag in this neighborhood at night?

I was not in the mood.

"Geez, I'm sorry I couldn't do more to help you out," Hal said, breathing hard. "Guess I'm not so fast on my feet anymore. You believe I used to be a pretty decent runner?"

He looked more like he used to be a department store Santa, but I didn't say that. The chance of him having a heart attack while racing after me was probably far greater than the chance of my catching the thief. I didn't say that either.

He was still puffing away. I thanked him for coming to the rescue, and he managed a grin. He had a round-cheeked face, a pointed chin, a widow's peak. His eyebrows were shaggy and graying, like his hair. Winded, he looked older than he had the night before.

"I never carry much cash," I said, as much to myself as to Hal. "It's the other stuff I mind. The license, the credit cards, the keys."

Hal said, "Your car keys? You be able to get home?"

"I'll take a cab," I said. "No problem."

"What are you gonna pay the cabbie with? I can spot you a twenty."

"Thanks," I said, "but no. I'll do okay." I keep a bill under the insole of my shoe like a lot of cops. Change in my pockets.

"So you were watching the show?" Hal said after half a block of silence.

"Dee invited me."

"Hey," he said, "no problem. Anything Dee says goes. She's something, isn't she? This new record, with the live cuts, it's gonna blow everything else out of the water."

We walked another silent block.

"How old is your daughter?" I asked, just to be saying something.

"Fifteen," he answered with a sigh. "They all want to be rock stars at fifteen."

I considered my little sister, Paolina. Just turned eleven and entering the dangerous age. Would she want to be a rock star too?

"So you're an old friend of Dee's," Hal said, still breathless but gamely keeping up his end of the conversation.

"You?" I asked in return. "You know her long?"

"Well, I started with her as a roadie back in the seventies. Worked for her off and on since then. I've carried her guitar through fifty states and most of Europe. She's always been square with me. Far as I'm concerned, creeps I've worked for, that qualifies her for sainthood."

"You're the road manager, right?"

"Yep."

"What is it you do?"

"Everything."

"You got an office with a phone?"

"You want to call the cops?"

"Just report my credit cards. Won't take long." All I have is my Harvard Coop card and Visa, and I wouldn't have Visa if it weren't for the rental car companies. Try to rent a car without a major credit card, and you've got yourself a hassle.

Hal said, "The Performance Center lets me use a hole-in-the-wall for the week. It hasn't got much, but it's got a phone. Hey, could you walk a little slower, maybe?"

"Sorry," I said. The guy couldn't have been more than five-five, with a barrel chest and short legs that were going twice as fast as mine. "Dee wanted to see me during the break."

"You play bass?" Hal said hopefully.

"Do I look like a bass player?" I asked.

"You look like a lady who answers all my questions with questions."

"Sorry," I said, which was not a question, but not an answer either.

"Dee will want to see me too," he said ruefully, after a brief pause. "She'll want Brenda's ass fried on a plate, and a fat slice of mine next to it. You'll see."

"She tough to work for?"

"Dee? Compared to most of the freaks in this business, no. And yeah, she's a bitch to work for."

He led me up a narrow flight of steps, concealed from the lobby by draperies, into an office so small there was barely room for both of us, a desk, and a filing cabinet. I did my phoning, which took twice as long as it should have. He shuffled some small slips of paper into an open drawer, closed it, and pretended not to listen.

"How do I get backstage?" I asked.

"Don't interrupt if they're playing, okay? I was kidding, you know, about wishing you were a bass player. This stuff with Brenda, it's happened before. Believe me, they love each other like sisters."

"Backstage," I said. "You're gonna tell me how to get there."

"Yeah." He gave me some fairly complex

directions. "And, listen, if you were my daughter, I'd add some advice."

"Such as?"

"Don't chase robbers. We've got a police force."

"I know," I said. "Thanks for trying to help me out."

"What did I do?" he protested, his grin shining through.

"Thanks anyway. You're up for the Good Samaritan of the Week award. And so far, there's not much competition."

CHAPTER ELEVEN

I followed Hal's directions through the lobby, back into the auditorium. Technicians were working onstage and Dee was nowhere in sight. I went through a draped doorway, up a steep short flight of stairs, and found myself surrounded by amplifiers and roadies. A hallway beckoned; I figured there had to be dressing rooms somewhere.

I located Dee's by the sound of her voice, opened the door after a cursory knock, and found her yelling at a tiny woman who was waving a needle and thread like a banner.

"I like the damn pants tight," Dee shouted at the seamstress. "If they split, they split."

"Wear clean underwear," I offered automatically. My mother used to say that: wear clean underwear in case you get hit by a car on the way to school. Think of the embarrassment if you have to go to the hospital in dirty underwear, or worse, with a safety pin holding your bra strap together.

It worries me when I find my mother's words coming out of my mouth.

"Where the hell have you been? I've been waiting half an hour." Dee rounded on me, and the tiny seamstress took the opportunity to escape. "I was counting on you to find Davey, find him fast," she went on angrily, not waiting for a response. She kicked off her heels, and four inches of white pant cuff brushed the floor.

"You know anybody who works with you and likes to steal ladies' handbags?" I asked.

"Huh?"

"Somebody ripped me off. Just now."

"You want to go call the police or something?"

"Does the building have security?" I asked.

"Oh, yeah," she said sarcastically. "Great security. Somebody tries to steal this building, I just bet the old-geezer patrol will notice."

"That good, huh?"

"I wouldn't leave a nickel in this dressing room. That's how good. I give everything to one of Hal's people. That handsome Jody guy, if I can find him. Now, you want to call the police or what?"

I sighed, and thought about all the Dumpsters and construction sites near Symphony Hall. "I'll take care of it later."

"You couldn't find Dunrobie?"

"Give me more time and — "

"Can I trust you?" she said suddenly, more like an accusation than a question.

I raised an eyebrow. "That depends, doesn't it?"

She reached inside her jacket, pulled an envelope out of the inner breast pocket, hefted it in her hand, and turned it over slowly. She bit her lower lip and tried to stare me down.

"Am I missing something?" I asked. "Because I like to have all the pieces before I play the game."

She started to speak, stopped, and closed her eyes. She looked drained, a different woman entirely from the electric wonder onstage.

"Whatever it is, Dee," I said, "whatever's going on, the music's fine. The music's terrific."

She didn't open her eyes, but she leaned against the closed door and started to talk. It seemed like she was talking to herself, but she must have realized I was still there, since she was blocking the only exit. "I worked my butt off to get where I am, and it bums me out that Dunrobie thinks he can pull this kind of shit." She stuck out her hand and gave me the envelope like she was glad to get rid of it.

It was standard size, embossed with the return address of a Stuart W. Lockwood, Esquire. Sent to Ms. Dee Willis, care of the Four Winds Hotel, 100 Boylston Street, Boston.

Typed at the bottom were the words "urgent and extremely personal." It had been neatly slit by a letter opener.

I unfolded a sheet of stiff paper. The attorney's name, address, phone, and fax were engraved top center. It was dated August 12. Three days earlier.

Dear Ms. Willis:

I represent Mr. David C. Dunrobie. Your recordings of "For Tonight," "Little Bit of Love," and "Jenny Lou" are based on his compositions "Sweet Lorraine," "Duet," and "Missing Notes."

You have failed to list Mr. Dunrobie as the composer of these songs, and you have further failed to list the songs under their original and correct titles. Your actions have deprived my client of his licensing fees and copyright payments, and constitute conversion of these songs to your own use.

"Sweet Lorraine," in particular, under your title, "For Tonight," has earned considerable remuneration, from recordings by other artists as well as yourself.

My client has suffered serious economic as well as emotional damage as a result of your conversion of his work. This matter requires your immediate attention. Please call me within the week and advise me how you intend to remedy this situation. If we have not heard from you by the close of business, August 19, 1991, my client has instructed me to proceed with enforcement of his rights under the law, including an injunction to prevent the performance and sale of these songs while this matter is in dispute. Litigation of these issues would necessarily involve other parties such as MGA/America, the manufacturers and distributors of *Change Up*.

I await your response.

Sincerely,
Stuart W. Lockwood, Esq.

I turned the page over; there was nothing on the back.

"Why the hell have I been chasing my tail all day?" I snapped. "Dunrobie's lawyer ought to know where he is."

"Do you believe this?" Dee grabbed the letter and waved it in my face before tossing it on the floor. She bent quickly and retrieved it.

"Happens all the time," I said. "You read about it in the papers. George Harrison stole

'My Sweet Lord' from so-and-so. Michael Jackson, all those people. You may not have realized you were doing it at the time, you just borrowed a riff here or there and whammo."

Dee glared at me. She spoke in an angry whisper, checking frequently to make sure the dressing-room door stayed shut. "If you don't believe me, nobody's gonna believe me. It's like this great American myth: If you're famous you steal things from the little guy." She clenched her fist, and then, not knowing what to do with it, let it fall to her side. "I am not going to have this happen to my life. I am not going to let Dunrobie do this to me."

"Is it too late to list him in the credits?"

"Davey Dunrobie never wrote one word or one note of any song I sing."

"So ignore it. Throw it away. Let him sue you."

She pulled over a rickety wooden chair, turned it backward, and sat on it. "Let me explain a few facts of life here, Carlotta. This could kill me. Really. You know for four whole years I couldn't get a studio to back me on an album? For four years, I'm like this fucking over-the-hill has-been. And those are the nice rejections. I put *my* money, damn near every dime, into *Change Up,* and I got Jimmy Ranger to mix it on spec. Now that

it's platinum for MGA/America, they're looking for a long-term contract. But with this
kind of shit, I don't know. I mean, MGA's
the deep pockets here. They can live without
a lawsuit."

"They'll shrug it off," I said. "You're making money for them, Dee."

"Listen to me," she said. "I'm not willing
to take the chance. I don't want them to hear
about it. I waited for a big label for ten years,
playing bars between catcalls, hauling ass
around the country, and earning enough to
eat. I want something to show for it besides
a scrapbook.

"There are *fifty* kids waiting out there for
my slot with MGA and any one of them could
be a major star with the right backing. Record
company execs eat their young, I swear to
God. Used to be, I never tried for a name.
Kind of songs I do aren't exactly top-ten material. I was born poor, I'm gonna die poor,
I told myself. Used to be, I just wanted to
make enough money to do what I'm doing,
play the music. But now I like my suite at
the Four Winds just fine. I like riding in lim-
ousines. And I keep thinking about those old
black guys, the bluesmen who taught me, the
ones who wound up in pine boxes with nothing."

"They were black," I said. "That had something to do with it."

"Yeah," Dee said. "And I'm a woman in a business where not many women front bands, write songs, choose their own arrangements, and play their own guitar."

"You gave me a whole song and dance about Dunrobie being a bum. Any of that true?"

"All of it."

"You talked to the lawyer?"

"I talked to him," Dee muttered. "He said to me, Davey wants three hundred thousand bucks."

I gave a low whistle.

"You need a lawyer," I said. "Lawyers like to duke it out with other lawyers. MGA's got lawyers earn more in an hour than I do in a month."

"Yeah, well, I hate lawyers," Dee said. "And MGA's lawyers aren't going to give a good goddamn about me. I want you. These new people, the ones who suck up to me and call me 'Miss Willis,' I don't trust any of them. They read my damn mail."

"Do they?"

"The *National Enquirer* hasn't printed anything about Dee Willis, song thief. Not yet."

"If you know what Dunrobie wants, and you know how to get in touch with his lawyer, what do you want from me? Why do you want me to find Davey?"

"Because the damn lawyer won't let me talk to him, says it would be — what did he say? — tantamount to harassing his client."

"Well, I'm not up on the fine points, but legally he may be right. Once suit is filed — "

She tapped the letter with a stubby fingernail. "You see anything in here about a suit being filed? I need to see Dunrobie before this goes any further."

"And you think if you talk to him, Davey will change his mind about the three hundred thousand, just like that?"

Dee nodded earnestly. *She thinks if she talks to a stone, she'll wear it down.*

She may be right. She talked me into another day's work.

CHAPTER TWELVE

"Detective Triola," I said.

"Hang on."

The police department doesn't try to soothe you with canned music while they keep you on hold. I appreciate that. Canned music makes me grind my teeth.

Joanne Triola and I went to the police academy together. She's still a cop, and I admire her for sticking it out. If you met her on the street, with her round gentle face and cloud of softly permed hair, you'd pick her for a librarian or a social worker. If you tried to shoot it out with her, you'd be dead.

"Triola," she said gruffly.

I said, "I'm looking for a cushy city job with short hours and long pay. A chance for a few bribes on the side. Have I got the right number?"

"What do you want, Carlyle?" she said. "Make it quick." She's good at recognizing voices.

"If you had your handbag snatched at Mass. Ave. and Boylston Street, kid took off toward Symphony Hall, where would you look for it?"

"You got your — "

"No gloating, Jo. Let's keep this hypothetical. Where are the regular dumps?"

On the whole, purse snatchers are creatures of habit, not leather fetishists. They don't collect handbags and wallets; they want money and credit cards. So when they get what they want, they dump the container as soon as possible, preferably in an unlighted alleyway or a convenient Dumpster.

"Hang on," Jo said. "I'll ask Rudy."

"Okay, write this down," Jo said when she got back on the line. She'd been gone so long I'd had to push five more dimes into the pay phone. "Alleyway behind the Amalfi. There's a Dumpster. Hope it's there."

I didn't like the way she said that. "Why?"

"Because the runner-up spot is the reflecting pool near the Mother Church."

"No," I said.

"Wear your rubber boots."

"I am not going wading tonight."

"Good. I wouldn't recommend it. Let me put out the word, and when somebody finds it I'll give you a call. Much cash?"

"Bastard didn't even get ten."

"Credit cards?"

"Harvard Coop. Visa. Period."

"Poor thief's sure sorry he picked you, lady."

"I'll grieve for him," I said, "while I'm standing in a three-mile line at the Registry getting a replacement driver's license. While I'm having new keys made."

"Yeah, it's a bitch," Jo said.

"And one more thing."

"Yeah?" Jo's voice was wary. I must have sounded a little too casual.

"There's a guy runs with the Gianellis. Mickey. Big Mickey something. I can't remember his last name. Eighteen-inch neck. Looks like an ex-football player. You know who I mean?"

"Vague memory."

"You know what line he's into?"

"Like drugs, prostitution, gambling, etcetera?"

"Like that."

"I'd have thought you'd be better placed to find out that sort of thing than I am."

"Jo," I said, "you ever call your boyfriend and ask him which of his dad's hoodlums runs broads? It's delicate."

"I'll see what I can find out," Jo said with a sigh. "And keep your hands on your purse at all times."

"Uh, Jo, could you do me a favor?"

"I thought that's what I was doing. Two favors."

"About the Gianelli thing?"

"Yeah?"

"Don't ask Mooney."

CHAPTER THIRTEEN

Stuart Lockwood, Esquire's office didn't look like his stationery. His stationery looked like money. His office looked like poverty. Single practice in downscale Somerville, shared space with a CPA. An orthodontist down the hall seemed to be the only one earning enough to gild the letters on his door.

Usually I visit law offices by appointment. I wear the closest thing I've got to a power suit, a navy blue number I picked up last year at a Filene's Basement close-out sale. After all, most of my high-paying clients are lawyers who want me to prove some dude was somewhere other than where the cops think he was last Saturday night.

I'd put on the navy blue for Lockwood, even though I had made no appointment, it was another steamer of a day, and he was an unknown quantity. I'd phoned a lot of friends and nobody could make him. The State Bar Association said he'd passed the North Dakota bar two years ago, the Massachusetts bar just last May. New boy on the block.

I'd been waiting outside his office door since eleven. No one had gone in or out. At eleven forty-five, I opened the door.

His secretary or paralegal or whatever, a thin blond kid in his early twenties, glanced up from an old swimsuit issue of *Sports Illustrated*.

"Hi," I said. "Mr. Lockwood in?"

Both inner office doors were closed. Behind one, I could hear someone talking. The voice droned on; it could have been a tape recording or a phone-message machine.

The lobby was six by ten and well-filled by a desk, a chair, and a low plaid couch that looked like it had come straight from the Salvation Army store. Framed prints of hunting dogs covered cracks in the plaster.

The young guy put his magazine down hastily, like I'd caught him red-handed.

"Do you have an appointment?" he asked, fumbling for a desk calendar.

"No," I said. "Mr. Lockwood was recommended to me by a friend at Palmer and Dodge."

"Oh," the kid said, impressed by the mention of one of the wealthiest practices in town. "Who?"

Palmer and Dodge has so many partners, you could pick a name out of the phone book. "Laura Breen," I said quickly. I'm sure he couldn't tell if I'd said Laura or Laurel, Breen or Green.

"Oh," he said again. "I'll see if Mr. Lockwood has a moment. You may have to wait."

"That's okay," I said. "Thank you."

The lobby didn't have a single magazine except for the *Sports Illustrated*. He didn't offer to share.

The kid disappeared into the office on the right and came back with a man older than I'd expected, someone who must have taken to the law later than the average student. He was runner-thin, graying. On second look, he seemed younger. The gray hair aged him.

He had a too hearty handshake, and a too toothy grin. He wore an elbow-rubbed blue shirt and baggy suit pants. He ushered me into an airless cube. His jacket and tie hung from a coat tree by a narrow window. The window was open, but didn't provide enough breeze to rustle the tie.

We established my name and his. The secretary lounged against the doorframe until he was dismissed.

Lockwood consulted his watch. Damned inconsiderate of somebody to call just before lunchtime. I concealed a grin at his irritation.

"I understand you represent David Dunrobie," I said.

"Where do you get your information?" he said. Trust a lawyer to respond with a question.

"A crystal ball," I said. "I see you giving me Dunrobie's address."

"Do you work for a collection agency?"

I've been called worse things. I gave him my card. Some people feel business cards prove your identity. The print shop never asks for my license when I order.

He stuck my card between the thumb and index finger of his right hand, tapped it on his desk. "Are you currently in the employ of an attorney?" he asked.

"Do I get to ask you a question if I answer that one?"

"Sit down, Miss, uh, Carlyle," he said.

"Thank you." There were only two chairs in the room: a worn easy-chair behind his desk and a guest chair that would have looked at home in a funky diner.

We studied each other for a while.

"You want me to divulge a client's address."

"I'd like you to write it down on a piece of paper," I said earnestly. "But I'll copy it if I have to."

"I'm sorry," he said. "You're wasting my time." He spoke as if he had a crowd of clients waiting on his sprung plaid sofa and cheap waiting-room chairs. Maybe he had a gold-mine practice, with billable hours to burn and no front. It's hard to tell.

"Mr. Dunrobie is an old friend," I said.

"Perhaps if you give him my card, he might get in touch with me. He might like to see me."

"I'll do that," he said.

I hadn't expected him to prolong the interview, any more than I expected Davey to drop by the next day.

We didn't shake hands when I left.

The one thing I'd managed to learn from my morning phone calls was that Mr. Lockwood would be unavailable after twelve o'clock today.

He exited the office soon after I did, still knotting his necktie. From a niche down the hallway, I saw him enter the elevator. I waited until I heard it descend.

Then I walked back up the hallway and opened the door.

"Oh." The kid was back into the swimsuit issue. He wasn't drooling, but close. "Forget something?" he asked.

"David Dunrobie," I said. "Does he live in Winchester or Woburn?" I showed him a small spiral-bound notebook. "I just wrote down a *W*. I'm almost sure it's Winchester, but I'd hate to drive all the way out there and then it's Woburn."

"No problem," the kid said generously.

He disappeared into Lockwood's office and I could hear him riffling through files. He carried a manila folder with him when he returned, but his face was closed and suspicious. Oh, well, a lot of towns around Boston begin with *W*. It could have worked.

"It's neither," he said. "What is this? You a server?"

He was sharper than I'd given him credit for. Maybe Lockwood did a lot of business with the avoid-a-subpoena crowd.

"You like music?" I asked, indicating the magazine. "Or just sports?"

I got the address in exchange for two comps to Dee's concert. Some things money can't buy.

"You sure about that?" I asked while I was writing it down.

"825 Winter Street. Boston," he said. "Suite 505D."

"It doesn't sound residential."

"It's all he's got. No phone, even."

I already knew that.

"Could you tell me if there's anything else in the file?" I asked.

"Nope," he said.

"There's nothing else, or you don't want to tell me. Which?"

"Got any more tickets?"

"I could manage one more," I said. "That's tops."

"An envelope," he said. "Sealed."

"Big? Little?"

"Eight by ten."

"Postmark?"

"Man, this is too weird," he said, closing the file and sliding it under the magazine. "I'm not telling you anything else."

"You don't have to," I said.

CHAPTER FOURTEEN

What with having to ditch the car — no one with more brains than a goose drives downtown — I didn't get to 825 Winter Street until a little past two in the afternoon.

Number 825 was an office building just like the ones on either side. A second-floor window advertised a realtor, a fourth-floor window a podiatrist. The remainder were unadorned. I noted the fifth floor particularly, figuring Suite 505D had to be on five, but it kept its secrets behind filmy curtains.

The lobby was cool and dark, marble-floored. There was no nameplate, no mail slot, for Suite 505D. There was, however, a Suite 500 with a doorbell. I pressed it, got an answering buzz, and entered. I ignored the old cage-elevator and righteously used the steps.

I'm no physical fitness nut, but I do play volleyball, the real kind, three days a week. Afterward, I swim. Today's match had taken longer than expected and I'd done only ten laps instead of my usual twenty. I took the steps to make up for it. Guilt is the major motivating force in my life.

High-pitched chatter leaked out under the

door marked 500. I checked all the doors on five, but there was no 505D. On the pebbled glass window of 500 I read the words "Hemstead Secretarial Services." I turned the knob and went inside.

The room couldn't have been more than eight by twelve, but there must have been eight women in it, one at each of the narrow, putty-colored desks, one to each twenty or so phone lines by the look of the complex switchboards. One wall was partitioned off into cubicles containing pieces of mail, brown-wrapped parcels as well as letters and brochures.

Each cubicle was numbered. 501A, B, C, 502A, B, C, and so on. No names.

A few of the women glanced up at me, but nobody seemed to be in charge. There was no receptionist's counter, no adjoining room. Hemstead, like Lockwood the lawyer, didn't put up much of a front. A phone rang.

I was still wearing my navy suit. Definitely overdressed for a visit to a mail drop.

"Mail drop" sounds so sinister, far worse than secretarial service. And a lot of people use them for perfectly legit purposes. Say your ex-husband regularly threatens to come by and check up on your morals; you might not want him to have your current address, especially if he outweighs your current beau by a hundred pounds and has a rep for using his fists. While you might choose not to announce your true address in the phone book, you might still wish to communicate with the outside world. So you have your mail sent to 825 Winter Street, Suite five-oh-whatever. Your "suite" is the little cubicle on the wall. When ex-hubby comes by to see who you're sleeping with, he won't get far.

Of course, a lot of the shady mail-order crowd use them too. I mean, would you rather send your money order to a post office box or to a street address in a good part of town, a suite number even? Suite conjures up such soothing imagery. Hotel suite. Doctor's office suite.

Post office box says beware. Red flag. Keep your money.

A woman in her fifties with frizzy brown hair, who'd been glaring around the office with a who's-going-to-take-care-of-this air, finally walked over to me.

"Can I help you?" she inquired with a martyr's sigh.

"Uh, I'm looking for Delores Fox," I said in my best airhead manner. "She still work here?"

"Delores?" The woman knitted her brow in concentration. "I don't think we've ever had a Delores. Not in the past three years anyway."

"Geez, I was sure she said the fifth floor," I mumbled. "I dunno. Maybe I got the address wrong."

"This is 825," the woman said helpfully.

I pawed through my substitute purse, an old navy leather bag I've never liked. "I know I got it in here somewhere. I just can't find it, and I thought I remembered . . ."

"Well, I have to get back to — "

"Sure. Sorry I interrupted. Thanks. I'll find her." I muttered my way out, grinning while I closed the door behind me.

I could have asked a lot of questions, but people who work for answering services and mail drops are trained not to answer inquiries about the clientele. Instead, I walked myself down Winter Street toward the Common, resisting the impulse to enter Filene's Basement to shop for shoes.

They rarely carry size 11's, but when they do, I stock up.

By the time I hit the Public Garden I was taking note of the picnickers lounging near the "Don't sit on the grass" signs, the popcorn vendors, and balloon hawkers. I stopped and bought a late-lunch hot dog slathered with mustard, and wolfed it down sitting on a park bench.

I tossed a leftover chunk of hot-dog bun to a squirrel with a ragged tail, got up, and dusted crumbs off my suit. The brazen squirrel made a beeline for them.

Why the hell would Dunrobie be using a mail drop? Was he homeless? If so, how the hell could he afford one? Had Lockwood, the lawyer, rented it for him so they could keep in touch?

I strolled back downtown.

On Washington Street, in front of Filene's, the city allows pushcart merchants to set up shop, hawking homemade jewelry, T-shirts, wind chimes, stained-glass dewdrops. One cart held a cargo of kites. A huge yellow one made me think of my little sister, Paolina. Yellow's her favorite color, so I bought it immediately. It made a long, skinny package, and the woman running the stand asked if I wanted a mailing tube. She had a stock of them in rainbow colors. I inspected them with growing enthusiasm, and finally chose a large matching yellow one. I let her put the kite inside. Then I selected another mailing tube, an even larger red one.

At the Arch Street post office, I addressed the yellow tube to Paolina, hoping her mother would let her keep the gift. Then I addressed the red mailing tube to Mr. David Dunrobie, 825 Winter Street, Suite 505D, etc., using Lockwood's Somerville office for the return address. I stood in line to mail them.

The man behind the counter disagreed with my decision to mail the red tube first-class. "This close," he urged, "you just send it regular parcel post and it'll get delivered day after tomorrow at the latest."

"If I send it first-class, will it go with tomorrow's delivery?"

"Sure," he said, "but it'll cost you two-forty instead of eighty-five cents."

I forked over the money for next-day delivery, feeling pretty damn good about my chances of tracking Davey. The glow lasted me through a Filene's Basement shoe spree — two pairs, a real haul — and a long walk to the Copley Square T station with frequent stops to stare at homeless men along the way. In Harvard Square, still feeling confident that Dunrobie was in the bag, I checked out the bill at the old Brattle Theater and decided impulsively to treat myself to a replay of *To Have and Have Not*.

Reality didn't catch up with me till I got home, hastily unlatched my three front-door locks, and raced into the living room in time to catch the ringing phone.

The voice was a whisper.

"Dee?" I said. "Is that you?"

"Oh, my God, oh, my God, oh, my God," the whisper said.

"Dee, where are you?"

"Oh, Carlotta."

"Where are you, Dee? Is anybody with you?"

"Come to the room, Carlotta. Oh, please come. I should have called the doctor. I should have stayed. I should have stayed."

I'd been looking forward to a very late dinner. I was glad I'd taken time to eat the hot dog in the park.

CHAPTER FIFTEEN

Dee's drunk, I told myself as I punched the button to summon the elevator. Stoned. Coked to a stupor. Or maybe just her usual melodramatic self.

No cops were camped in the hotel lobby; the disaster couldn't be that bad.

That's what I said to myself, but I practically stood on my toes to speed the elevator, and I hurried down the silent eighth-floor corridor. Then I paused for a moment, unsure which of the suite's doors to bang. I picked 812 — the living room, I thought — knocking softly, restraining my volume with effort. No need to cause a disturbance unless one was already under way.

"Oh, for chrissakes, uh, uh, who is it?" stammered a startled voice.

I said, "Carlyle. Dee called me."

I could hear the buzz of arguing voices. I hit the door again, harder. "Come on," I said. "Open up."

"Shhh." The door eased open a cautious three inches. Mimi, the blonde groupie, frowned and reluctantly let me pass.

Dee was seated in the center of a white sofa,

her face pale and blank, her arms crossed like she was warding off a chill. Her hands moved restlessly, squeezing her bare arms. She wore black. It looked like a silk jumpsuit, but it could have been pants and a matching sleeveless shirt. Beads spilled down her chest, gold like the ones scattered in the park. "Oh, my God," she murmured without looking up. "My God. What time is it?"

"Shhh," a man said, "hush, now." But Dee spoke over his voice as if he hadn't said a thing.

"Where were you all?" she said, still without looking up. "I should have called a doctor. Oh, God, I should have called a doctor. Maybe she isn't dead."

"Dead?" I echoed.

Jimmy Ranger had been pointed out to me at the party. I recognized him as the man who was trying to shush Dee. Before he got to be one of the hottest record producers around, he'd sung a little blues himself. I'd seen him on a double bill with Taj Mahal at the Sanders Theater in Cambridge. He had hair then. Now he had shoulder-length fringe surrounding a bald spot. He ignored me and said, "You've got to stop this, Dee. Pull yourself together."

Hal Grady smiled weakly from a kneeling position near Dee's feet. He wore a T-shirt emblazoned across the back with *Change Up*,

THE TOUR. He said, "We've got to consider the public relations angle here."

"Carlotta," Dee said, breathing quickly and shallowly, "he's just trying to scare me. I know he's trying to scare me."

"Is somebody going to give me a clue?" I asked slowly, biting off each separate word.

The road manager exchanged a long glance with the record producer. Then he nodded toward the connecting door that led to the bedroom with the canopied gold bed. "You got a sensitive stomach?" he asked.

I was already moving.

Brenda, the dark-haired bass player with the strong handshake and the short fuse, lay across the bed, her skin so pale, it seemed a shade of blue. The sheet almost covered her bare shoulders. Her face looked like it had been carved in ice.

Both times I'd seen her, at the party in Dee's room and on the Berklee stage, she'd been commanding, assured. Now she seemed delicate, almost frail.

Just shorter lying down, I said to myself. Snap out of it. You've seen corpses before. I rested my knuckles lightly against her throat. No pulse. I hadn't expected one.

I never get used to it, the unknowable mystery of a person so suddenly, totally closed, snapped shut like a half-read novel.

I tucked my hands into the pockets of my suit jacket. Reflex. Mooney used to make the uniforms grab a pencil and a notebook. If you weren't toting a notebook, you stuck your hands in your pockets.

I'm no compulsive housecleaner, but I always feel a tug to touch something at a crime scene, to tidy away a cigarette butt, to smooth a tangled curl. Maybe it's just a way of pinching myself to make sure I'm awake.

On the marble-topped bedside table sat a squat bottle of tequila, a drinking glass, two prescription pill bottles. One glass. No lipstick on the rim. Brenda's wire-rimmed glasses. A copy of *Guitar* magazine. The cover had wet circles on it, as if it had been used as a coaster.

The white sheet had frilly lace edging.

"You cover her?" I found that Jimmy Ranger had followed me into the room, so I addressed the question to him.

"We didn't touch anything," he said defensively.

"You use that phone?"

"Uh, I guess Dee did. Yes. To call you."

"You were here when she called?"

"Yeah. Sure. We all got back to the room together." He stared me right in the eye.

"Who's all?"

"Me. Hal. Mimi and Freddie. I think Ron was with us. Yeah. We didn't see why everybody should wait. Ron and Freddie were whacked-out. They went to bed."

"And since then you've been sitting on the sofas, probably using the bathroom."

"Uh, yeah."

"You find somebody dead," I said harshly, because I hate being lied to, "you get out of the room. If you're alone, you call for help. If there are two of you, one stands guard, the other calls for help."

"Yeah," he said, "I'll remember that the next time I find a corpse."

"How long since you called the cops?"

"Uh, we, uh — we've been thinking what to do. Dee thought maybe you could, uh — "

"So your bass player's dead in your lead singer's bed, and you're sitting around holding a panel discussion about PR implications?"

"Don't get snotty with me," he said. "It sure ain't gonna matter to Brenda whether she died in this bed or her own."

I said, "I have to use the phone."

"No," he said.

"What are you going to do? Stop me?"

"Please, honey, call the doctor." Dee entered from the other room on unsteady legs, followed closely by Hal. "I should have called. I should have called. Maybe she was still alive." She stumbled and Hal helped her into a chair. She leaned her head over, forehead to knees, and clasped her thighs, rocking in silent misery. "He did this," she muttered. "He's trying to ruin me."

"Shh, now," the road manager murmured soothingly.

A white phone was perched on a white desk, just like in the living room.

"Don't touch a damn thing while I'm gone," I ordered, thinking how useless the words were even as I said them. I used a fold of my shirt to cover the door handle on my way out. There was a maid's cart two doors down. My Spanish was good enough to convince her to let me into an empty room.

It had a white phone too. I dialed 9 first to get a dial tone. I considered 911, punched Mooney's number instead. In Massachusetts, nobody's dead until they've been pronounced dead by a medical examiner, but in my opinion Brenda no longer rated emergency status. After I gave Mooney the outline, I added, "No sirens, okay?"

That's what the uniforms say when they find a dead politician in a strange bed.

I hung up. The maid, reluctant to leave me alone in the unoccupied room, regarded me with stony eyes.

"When did you make up 812?" I asked, fumbling with the numbers in Spanish.

She nodded a few times, then spat back a

torrent about the loco music people, how they sleep all day, party all night, and never get out of the rooms, so she can't do her work. They leave dishes in the bathtub. Broken dishes. Her eyes flashed as if she were glad some retribution had justly struck.

This time I knocked on the bedroom door. Mimi, like a faithful attendant, let me in. I wondered who she'd been with tonight. Probably the now sleeping Freddie. Jimmy Ranger? The lead guitar, Ron? Or was he Dee's main action? Chunky little Hal? Would a road manager have the glamour to attract Mimi? Would she work him into a free evening so he'd let her backstage whenever he was touring a show?

Hal was patting Dee's hand when I came in, comforting her like a child. "She's suffering from shock," he announced, stepping between us like some knight in aging armor. "She doesn't know what she's saying."

I asked, "When did you really get here? Not till after Dee called me, right?"

Jimmy Ranger said, "Shut up." His warning glance included everyone in the room.

I wondered if last night's rehearsal had proceeded without the bass player. Had Brenda relented, come back? And without her, how would the tour go on?

"If that's your line," I said to the gnome,

"about her not knowing what she's saying, you'd better get a tame doctor in here and keep her from chatting with any cops."

Hal exchanged a brief glance with Jimmy Ranger and walked to the desk with commendable speed.

"Not that phone," I snapped. "Matter of fact, it would be better if we all got out of this room."

The road manager knelt in front of Dee; tilted her chin so she'd see him. "Don't say anything till I get back, Dee, honey," he said softly.

Dee raised her eyes to me. "You know," she said tremulously.

I didn't, but I went over and helped her to her feet. I figured if I got her back onto the white sofa, the rest would follow like sheep. The fewer visitors to the scene of a crime the better. The shorter the duration of each visit the better. As I walked Dee through the connecting doors I murmured, "Does this mean you want me to keep doing what I'm doing? Looking for Davey?"

"No," she said quickly, her hand to her throat. "Oh, no. Just let it be. Please. I never should have started this. Oh, poor Bren." She got a funny faraway look on her face. "Oh, God. Oh, God. I should have called the doctor."

"Cut the crap, Dee," Ranger said. "At least cut it when the cops get here. We all got here together. And she was dead. She was ice-cold."

This from a man who'd assured me he'd touched nothing.

He went on, but whether he was talking to Dee, or for my benefit, I wasn't sure. "She killed herself, that's bad enough. Don't, for chrissake, make it worse."

I got Dee settled on the sofa. Mimi sat on the carpet, wide-eyed, spacey. The others used furniture.

"Dee," I said, "you think there's something funny here, you tell the cops."

"And kiss the tour good-bye, Dee," Ranger said. "Kiss the MGA/America deal good-bye."

Dee put her hands over her ears.

Ranger muttered, "If it wasn't her room, the damage would be minimal. Brenda was in a funk. Everybody saw her walk out of rehearsal. Nobody could find her the whole damned day. And Dee's talked about replacing her before."

The hall door opened, and we all jumped involuntarily. Hal breezed in, a glow of achievement on his face. Before he could report his success at finding a willing physician, Ranger asked, "Is the room in Dee's name, or the tour's name? Do we have a block, Hal, or is this room specifically in her name?"

"Block," Hal said, after a moment's thought.

"Let's get Dee moved out quick. Somebody — Freddie or Ron — can move his stuff in — "

"The hell with that," Mimi said, leading me to believe she was sharing the drummer's room, and maybe not as stoned as she appeared to be.

"Right," I said. "You give the best room in the hotel to the drummer, and Dee Willis has to stick her stuff in the broom closet. The cops will buy it easy."

"Cops are dumb."

"Yeah, except I didn't call the dumb ones."

"Gee, thanks," Hal said sarcastically.

"Before the dumb cops get here, can somebody tell me the story?" I asked.

"There's no story," Ranger insisted. "We walked in, we sat down, we were gonna order from room service. Dee, or maybe it was Mimi, peeked in the bedroom and said, 'Hey, they haven't cleaned up the room yet,' or something like that, because the bed wasn't made. Then we, uh, we saw it, saw what happened."

"Who went in first?" I asked.

Nobody answered.

"Dee, why don't you lie down on the couch?" Hal quickly filled the silence. "The doctor will be here in a minute or two. It'll look better if you lie down."

"What?" Dee said, plainly bewildered. "Oh, God, Bren, I'm so sorry." She hunched over and her shoulders started to shake.

The cops beat the doctor by seven minutes.

CHAPTER SIXTEEN

The first team — a uniform I didn't know and an older plainclothes I remembered — showed up with the hotel manager in tow. She had to be the manager; no lowly desk clerk could afford her snakeskin heels, much less her suit. Totally unruffled, she breezed down the hall as if a dead bass player or two were all in a day's work. With her help, the cops quietly commandeered the bedroom and living room of Dee's suite as well as the adjoining function room where the MGA/America stiffs had partied two nights ago.

That's where they sent the witnesses to wait.

The room had been transformed. It was sedate, ready for a high-society wedding. The Mylar balloons had disappeared along with the rock band setup. Twelve linen-covered round tables ringed the dance floor. Mimi sat alone at a table for eight until Freddie, blinking and looking hastily roused from sleep, joined her. Jimmy Ranger and Hal Grady huddled at another table, their balding heads close together. I could hear them mumbling in low tones. The lead guitar, Ron, came in, still buttoning his shirt, and I marveled at how close he was in build to my ex-husband, Cal. Dee and I just liked the same sort of men. I thought about introducing myself to Ron, but he quickly surveyed the room and joined Freddie and Mimi. Nobody invited me to rub elbows, and I found myself too restless to sit. I wanted to reexamine the scene of Brenda's death, ask Dee a few questions. Alone.

Like why I should stop looking for Davey Dunrobie.

Like who had arranged the invitations for the MGA bash and included Mickey on the list.

Like exactly what Lockwood had said on the phone besides three hundred thousand bucks.

Like whether she'd be willing to swear on something she held holy, like the Reverend's guitar, that she'd really written "For Tonight."

I paced a narrow track by the windows, staring down at the lights that sparkled the trees on Boston Common. If the windows could have been opened, I would have opened one just to hear a car honk, a siren wail, anything to break the heavy silence of the room.

Instead I walked faster, clacking my heels against the parquet floor.

I wondered where Dee was, whether the road manager's quack would keep her from mumbling that she should have called the doctor because maybe stone-cold Brenda was still alive.

The young cop summoned Mimi first, then Freddie, then Ron, then Ranger, then Hal Grady. I wondered if I'd have drawn a lower number wearing the hotel manager's charcoal suit and cream silk blouse.

When the uniform finally ushered me in, he and his partner were remarkably polite, as if the atmosphere of the hotel had rubbed off on them. Cops find a junkie overdose in Grove Hall, they treat it differently than a drink-and-pills in a posh hotel. I heard no references to meat wagons, no discussion of the anatomical attributes or shortcomings of Brenda's body.

I wondered how the detectives who'd investigated Lorraine's long-ago suicide had gone about it. Had they been influenced by her fleabag Jamaica Plain digs? Seen her as one more skinny hippie-chick OD? No cop had asked me any questions about her death. But then, I hadn't been at the scene.

Mooney showed up, and for a brief time we were all buddies together. The old guy realized he did know me from way back — he never forgot a face, by God — and you know, they had a whole lot more women cops now. From the way he said it, I was pretty sure he didn't approve of the change.

Mooney told me to wait a minute, and he and the two cops slipped through the connecting hall to the bedroom. They left both doors ajar. I'd had my fill of waiting, so I followed. Lightning seemed to flicker from the bedroom, but I figured it for a photographer snapping shots of Brenda's body. I peered through the doorway, not really trying to eavesdrop.

"Might as well come on in, Carlotta," Mooney said.

A slew of cops was present and busy, taking inventory with gloved hands, shooting photographs, dusting for prints. Maybe the hotel had a special arrangement with the police department: quick and efficient service in exchange for respectable corpses.

Brenda's was still covered by the sheet. The pile of clothes by the side of the bed was presumably hers.

The medical examiner arrived, and I was glad Mooney motioned me out into the hall. This particular M.E.'s sense of humor — a job requirement, I suppose — always made me gag.

"Are you working for Dee Willis?" Mooney asked. He didn't pull out a notebook, but I didn't take it for a casual question. He's got a memory like a lockbox.

"No," I said with a clear conscience. Dee had made it perfectly plain that she no longer wanted me to find Dunrobie. I always like to tell Mooney the truth.

"But she phoned you to come over? Before she called the police?"

He must have gotten a quick summary from the cops inside. "It sounded urgent. She was upset. If I'd known anybody was dead, I'd have phoned you from my house."

"When she called you, did you get the impression she was alone?"

"I couldn't see a thing over the line," I said flatly.

"Seriously," he said.

"Seriously," I said.

He wasn't happy with my reply. He switched gears. "Tell me about the park," he said.

"You talk to the officers involved?" I was sure he had.

"You see any connection between the park and this, uh, unexpected death?" he asked.

What had Dee mumbled? Something about somebody trying to scare her. Could she have meant Dunrobie?

I didn't think Mooney could see my face. The light in the hallway was dim.

"If you're not going to tell me anything, why did you call me?" he asked mildly. He talks that way when he's just starting to get angry.

"To keep it low-key," I said. "Dee's an old friend. She's worked hard for what she's got, and she doesn't need a lot of nasty publicity."

"You can't keep murder that quiet," he said.

"Who's talking murder?" I said.

"Come on. Don't tell me you didn't look around in there."

"A quick glance," I admitted.

"You didn't touch anything?"

"Damn straight I didn't."

"So?"

"So it's very neat," I said reluctantly.

"You want to try and tell the medical examiner she didn't vomit up any of that stuff, didn't thrash around, just laid herself out like she was ready for the funeral director to decorate her with lilies?"

I said, "And then there are the circles on the magazine."

"You can come back to work anytime," Mooney said. "Two different sizes, two different glasses. Where's the other glass?"

I shrugged.

"Let me run this by you. Your friend Dee scores some dope in that park. She and the bass player decide to play some bed games, drink some booze, take some pills. Dee maybe falls asleep, and when she wakes up, she can't wake Brenda. So she cleans house and calls you."

"Whoa," I said. "First of all, trust me, no drugs in the park. Then what do you figure? Dee changed the sheets? What did she use to clean up with? Think she carries a can of Ajax? You see a bunch of used towels any-place? Dirty sheets?"

"I don't think there's much that road man-ager wouldn't do to smooth this tour. That record producer, either. Everybody seems like they want to do Dee Willis a favor. Even you."

"Oh, I get it. You think she called me to bring over a mop and a vacuum cleaner."

"Don't get mad," he said.

"It's late. Maybe she died somewhere else and somebody moved her here," I said. "What's wrong with that?"

"Just walked the stiff through the halls? It's kinda early for Halloween."

"Brenda and Dee had a pretty public ar-gument last night," I said. "I think Dee may have fired her."

"And?" Mooney said.

"So maybe she decided she didn't want to look for another job. Took a bunch of pills, couldn't remember how many, took some more, had a few drinks. Died."

"In her own hotel room, I might buy it.

But who moved her? And why?"

I said, "Isn't this where the cops always look for the significant other?"

"Finding her in Willis's bed sort of made me forget she might be married. Was she?"

"I'm not talking marriage, Mooney. I'm talking sleeping with, and she was very cuddly with a guy first time I saw her."

"What guy?"

"Five-six, slight, dark eyes, dark hair. Freddie, the drummer, called him her 'boy-toy,' and Brenda didn't appreciate the term one bit. He was a kid. Couldn't be more than twenty-two, twenty-three."

"This 'boy-toy' have a name?"

"Haven't the faintest. You finished here?"

"You can go," Mooney said, "if that's what you're asking."

"Can I talk to Dee?"

"They moved her down the hall. I think a doctor's in there asking for her autograph."

"Yeah, you think I can talk to her?"

"Doctor says no."

Hal must have gotten somebody good.

Mooney said, "If you manage to talk to her, you're not gonna come out and tell me what she said, are you?"

"No," I said.

"I can't force you to tell me," Mooney said.

"I'm glad you're clear on that."

"What about a favor?" Mooney asked. "A return on letting her walk after that park crap."

"What do you want to know?" I said cautiously.

"While you were waiting for the cops to come, you hear Miss Willis say anything odd?"

"Odd?" I tossed the word back at him.

"Something like, 'I should have called the doctor. She might have been alive. . . .'"

"Would that be odd?" I asked.

"Considering the lady's been dead for hours and the other people in the room all say they never even thought about a doctor, yeah, I would say that's a little odd. Makes you think maybe Dee was there before the others. Since it's her room, she might have come back earlier than the rest. . . ."

"Going fishing?" I asked Mooney.

"And I wonder how this dead woman got into the room. They've got those card-keys, supposed to be pretty secure."

"I was here the other night, after the park business, and a whole crowd was partying in Dee's room. Got a duplicate key at the desk. No questions asked."

"Interesting," Mooney said. "And I hear you lost your handbag."

I hoped Jo had kept her mouth shut about Mickey. I didn't need Mooney riding me about my relationship with a known Gianelli.

"Yeah," I said.

"Did it turn up in any of the dumps?"

"Not that I've heard," I said. "Not yet."

"Keys in the bag?"

I nodded.

"Change the locks yet?"

"No, Mom, but I'm gonna put Roz right on it."

"Good."

"So can I see Dee?"

"Sure. If you can get past the doc."

I gave up after twenty-five minutes. Reporters, probably tipped off by somebody in the hotel, were starting to swarm up the elevators.

I stayed long enough to watch the well-groomed hotel manager escort Brenda's unfashionably bagged body down a service elevator. God forbid a tourist should be confronted by the grim reaper in the lobby.

CHAPTER SEVENTEEN

The phone shrilled while I was mid-dream, so I incorporated its jangle into a bizarre scenario involving Dee, Mooney, my ex-husband, Cal, and me, in which the four of us raced through hotel corridors, popping in and out of doorways like cartoon characters. The rules, reminiscent of musical chairs, were strict: whoever lacked his or her own room when the phone stopped ringing would be in deep trouble — or else something quite erotic would happen, something involving Dee's gold four-poster bed and several silky red scarves.

I woke with the telephone receiver in my hand, so I put it to my lips and muttered hello.

"Is this the Carlyle Detective Agency?" The voice was male and extremely well-bred, a bit British in its intonation.

"Yes," I said, leaning back on a pillow. Sunlight streamed through my thin bedroom curtains. I glanced at the clock-radio on the bedside table and saw it was past nine, almost nine-thirty. I'd overslept.

"Miss Carlyle?"

I prefer Ms., but I grunted acquiescence.

"Taylor Baines here. I'm an attorney with Barlow, James, and Hunt. Retained by MGA/America."

"Yes," I said again, because he'd stopped talking.

"It would be far better to speak in person."

"Concerning a certain singer?"

"Yes."

I said, "What time?"

"Can you make it at eleven?"

"Where?"

"Number One Beacon Street. The twenty-second floor."

I scribbled on the back of an envelope.

"Eleven o'clock," I said. As soon as I hung up, I found the phone book and dialed the Four Winds. I asked for Dee Willis, rather than room 812. No cop or doctor would let Dee spend the night in that gold-swagged bed. The receptionist informed me that Miss Willis was unavailable. I tried for Jimmy Ranger or Hal Grady, and got the same response, the all-purpose publicity freeze.

I wondered how Dee was handling Brenda's death this morning. I checked to see how I was handling it, and was surprised to find I was angry. Angry at death? Pretty presumptuous of me. Angry, I supposed, that no one but Dee seemed to care. What the hell was wrong with someone like Jimmy Ranger, who seemed to see Brenda's death only as a possible roadblock to the tour? What about Hal? Mimi, the groupie? Freddie? The unflappably cool guitarist, Ron. I remembered them all, dry-eyed and unshocked, as if they lost a band member once a month, as if Brenda were some plastic mannequin who adorned the stage and struck the occasional chord.

I swung my feet onto the cool wooden floor, and remembered the night I'd heard about Lorraine's death. I was getting dressed for a party — I still had the dress I'd been planning to wear tucked away in a closet somewhere — and I'd kept on applying mascara to my lashes, adjusting my stockings, combing my hair — carefully, very carefully, as if each separate grooming act were important, gravely important, even though I no longer had any intention of going to the party.

I didn't cry until six hours later.

Maybe the band deserved a break. Maybe they hadn't processed the information yet.

I wondered how long Brenda had been part of the group. When had Dee become discontented with her playing? Maybe Brenda was a new addition. Maybe Dee would brush it off.

But what the hell had she meant by "He did it; he's responsible"? Had the Dunrobie letter made her so nervous that she'd yelled at Brenda more than usual? Did she think that

Davey had somehow tricked Brenda into over-dosing for the sole purpose of throwing a scare into Dee?

Did she think Davey had poisoned a gin and tonic and left it on her bedside table for Brenda to come along and swig by mistake? I'd ruled mistaken identity out from the start. Two circles on the magazine meant two glasses, two people. And any fool could dis-tinguish the tall, big-boned Brenda from the delicate Dee.

Dee had been clear about one thing; she didn't want me to continue the Dunrobie search.

I wondered about the lawyer's call; what kind of trouble was Dee in now? I wondered what combination of drink and drugs had fin-ished Brenda.

I staggered across the hall to the shower and stood under its stinging spray, washing my hair because it needed it. The water turned icy before I finished rinsing.

I dressed quickly, in my reliable navy suit again, choosing a silk shirt this time to match the lawyer's upscale address. Its notched col-lar looked fine with my aunt Bea's gold locket.

My bold fashion statement for the year is this: clothes cost too damn much money, and shopping for cheap good clothes takes too damn much time. And even if you find your dream outfit, the washer and dryer eat it alive, or you're condemned to continually ransom it from the dry cleaner.

I don't own a lot of clothes. I maintain you can make do with the same stuff over and over if you use the occasional scarf and change your shoes and jewelry. Not that I own much jewelry.

Fortunately, my tenant, Roz, has glitz enough for both of us. She was standing at the refrigerator door, pondering either breakfast or the meaning of life. Her hair, bleached and colored more often than I shampoo, was coal-black with a central white stripe. She looked not unlike a skunk. I wondered if she'd made a mistake and changed her mind halfway through the dye job.

She turned at the sound of my footsteps. Her necklace, looped over a torn black turtleneck, looked like it had been soldered together from beer-can tab-pulls. Each of her fingers was ringed. I'm used to the six studs in her left ear. Her right varies. Today she sported what looked like two strands of neon hanging from tiny chicken bones.

I don't wear earrings. They hurt. And I think they're just plain silly.

"Can you do a job for me?" I asked. "Two jobs."

"Today?"

"Is that a problem?" Roz has a heavy schedule, which involves making the scene at several rock clubs, and painting pictures that seem stranger the longer you look at them.

"What is it?"

"First, call a locksmith, and have the locks changed. Not all of them, just one on each door." If the thief came calling, which I doubted very much, I'd enjoy catching him in the act.

"Okay," Roz said, "then what?"

"Surveillance."

"Boring," she said, turning back to refrigerator inspection.

"Money," I reminded her.

"Better than cleaning, I suppose."

The way my house looks, Roz obviously thinks anything is better than cleaning. I always mean to sit her down and explain the basics, like you sweep the kitchen floor before you mop it, but somehow I can never bring myself to start the lecture.

I gave her the Winter Street address, told her to stick to anyone who left the building carrying a red mailing tube, not to lose the tube, to get the license plate of anyone who picked it up in a car, to follow the car —

"I could do this better with Lemon," she interrupted.

Lemon is her karate instructor and sometime lover, although Roz is not the monogamous type. He owns a dark green van, a great surveillance vehicle. Roz doesn't drive, and I often think she keeps up her self-defense lessons so she can have a set of wheels at her disposal.

I said, "No fooling around in the van while the mailing tube walks."

"Red," she said. "It won't get by me."

One thing about Roz: being an artist, she knows her colors.

I took the T to One Beacon Street.

During the train ride, I tried to read the *Globe* without elbowing the passenger sitting beside me, or socking anybody standing in the aisle. Brenda's death hadn't made the obituary column, much less Metro news. I wondered where the bass player came from and who'd been notified as next of kin.

I finished reading and stared critically at my blackened hands. I swear the quality of newsprint declines daily. The lawyer with the nice British voice was going to get a surprise if he offered to shake hands.

I found a coffee shop in the lobby, followed the signs to the restroom, and scrubbed the ink off. Then I rushed back to the elevators and rode up to the twenty-second floor.

CHAPTER EIGHTEEN

"This is a little awkward," Taylor Baines admitted with a charming smile after releasing my clean hand. I sat in a caramel-colored leather chair that commanded a view of Boston harbor through a huge picture window. The ocean looked smooth as glass, green as a 7-Up bottle.

He was a small, dapper man, late forties by the crow's-feet at the corners of his eyes, older by the silver hair. Impeccably dressed in a navy suit with a fine gray stripe, the proper amount of white shirt-cuff peeped out of his sleeves. His gold wristwatch was thin as a dime.

He sat behind a desk that was twice as big as my dining room table.

He asked if I'd take coffee. I said yes, cream and sugar, please. He small-talked until a woman appeared with a tray and two china cups. Saucers and silver spoons too. He neatly segued into business as soon as the door swung shut behind her.

"I represent MGA/America, which currently has an interest in Miss Dee Willis. You are a, uh, friend of hers."

It wasn't a question so I didn't answer it.

Taylor Baines stirred his coffee and waited for me to explain my relationship with Dee. One corner of his mouth tilted up when I said nothing.

"You are also a private investigator licensed by the Commonwealth of Massachusetts," he said.

I nodded.

"Miss Willis has taken a rather unfortunate tone with the police, concerning an accident which occurred at her hotel last night, involving a member of her entourage."

I made a noncommittal noise.

"I am told that she has been both too forthcoming and too closemouthed in her interactions with the police department, and that she runs the risk of getting herself and her tour, which is financed entirely by our client, into some, er, difficulty."

"May I ask what she allegedly told the police?"

My use of "allegedly" drew another faint tilt of the attorney's mouth. "Miss Willis has said that she knows the death was not suicide, but that she can tell them no more than that. She knows because she knows, in other words."

"Maybe they won't take her too seriously," I offered. "When I was a cop, we had psychics who called long-distance to discuss the reappearance of Elvis."

"Yes, but Miss Willis also maintains that she found the, uh, body in the company of a group of her fellow musicians, and that she has no idea why the body was in her room."

I said nothing.

"The police say they have received differing accounts of the body's discovery. I understand Miss Willis telephoned you from the scene."

I said nothing again.

"MGA/America is most anxious that her tour continue unimpeded."

"If Dee isn't being held for questioning, is there any reason why it shouldn't?"

Mr. Baines stole a quick glance at his watch. "She is, at the moment, resting at her hotel. The hotel switchboard will say she is unavailable."

He was certainly right about that. I finished my coffee, which was very good, and set the delicate cup and saucer on the corner of his desk. "Why am I here?"

"Ah," he said. "I am to assure you that MGA/America will be happy to cover your usual fee for whatever, uh, service you are supplying to their artist."

"And in return for the money, what do they want?"

"First of all, they would like you to continue

working for Miss Willis."

"Who says I'm working for Ms. Willis?" I said. "We are old friends."

"The best kind," he said.

"Yes," I agreed. "The best kind."

He said, "I did tell the client I felt this sort of thing would be a waste of time."

"No problem," I said evenly. "It might have been a problem if I were working for Ms. Willis, but I'm not."

"Ah," he said. "That makes things somewhat easier. You would then be free to accept another job?"

"I might."

"Miss Willis approached someone at MGA/America early this morning concerning the loan of a considerable amount of money."

"May I ask how much?"

"Three hundred thousand dollars. As an advance against royalties on a recording contract. Up until this morning, contract negotiations were proceeding at a somewhat leisurely pace. Miss Willis seems to wish to speed the process along. And my clients, before signing any documents, particularly large checks, would feel more secure if someone like you were present to keep an eye on Miss Willis, to speak to her perhaps, to urge her to use more tact in her conversations with the police."

"I would hardly be able to keep her from

telling them the truth," I said.

"No," he agreed, with the faintest hint of a smile. "But we feel, that is, my clients feel, that Miss Willis should have a discreet friend to rely on at this upsetting time."

"You can't hire a friend," I said. "But if I were to wish to speak with someone at MGA/America concerning Ms. Willis, who would that someone be?"

"You can always reach me at one of these numbers," he said smoothly, removing a thin leather case from the inside pocket of his suit jacket. We traded business cards. I got the better of the deal; his — thick, cream-colored, engraved — probably cost three times as much as mine.

"I admire your view," I said.

"If you should happen to come across anything that would convince the police that Miss Willis was elsewhere at the time of Miss Hunter's death, MGA/America would appreciate knowing it. Will a retainer of five hundred be sufficient?"

I nodded. "Has Dee been charged with anything?"

"No."

"Are you anticipating she will be?"

"There remains that possibility."

Behind his head to the right, I could see a tugboat escorting a freighter out to sea. I couldn't make out the name on the bow, but I thought it might be in the Cyrillic alphabet. If I had an office with a view like that, I don't think I'd get a lick of work done.

CHAPTER NINETEEN

Walking through the Common, following the meandering paths from Park Street Station to Charles Street, I sorted it out. Two days ago, Dee had been dead set against paying Dunrobie a dime. This morning she wanted to float a loan — and for the exact amount Davey hoped to extort.

And in between? Brenda's death.

From Taylor Baines's earnest request, it sounded like someone at MGA/America was pretty sure Dee was in deep trouble and hoped I could help her out.

Or else someone at MGA/America wanted to find out if their new sensation was up to her knees or her neck in hot water.

Either way, I'd been hired for damage control, to report back with whatever dirt I could dig. That was MGA/America's message, and Taylor Baines was the high-class messenger boy.

I wondered who'd pointed the record company in my direction.

I patted the folded check in my pocket. I was glad I'd followed my gut and sent Roz to keep an eye on the mailing tube. Now I could afford to ignore Dee's dismissal, to keep looking for Davey Dunrobie.

I walked faster, shucking my jacket in the blazing heat, draping it across my arm. I wished my silk shirt had short sleeves. With silk, roll the sleeves, and you have to iron the wrinkles out. I'm a menace with an iron, and Roz is not much better.

One thing about Roz as a housemate: I'm never tempted to borrow any of her clothes. Maybe I could do a hell of a job for Taylor Baines and afford a short-sleeved silk blouse as well as a new purse. The cops hadn't found my bag in any of the likely dumps. If it didn't turn up soon, I'd have to go through the dreaded driver's license replacement rigamarole. By that time, I'd probably have frittered Baines's money away on car repairs, taxes, cat food. The little luxuries.

"I should have called the doctor. She might not have been dead." And then, later, "He did it. He's trying to scare me." I mumbled Dee's words to myself as I walked, the same way I used to memorize songs back in the days of our group, Cambridge Common. It's okay to eyeball the lyrics at rehearsal, Lorraine or Dee would lecture, but during performance, you better know it cold.

There are public phones galore in the new Copley Square park. The trick is finding an unvandalized one. It took me three tries, but I finally located one, punched my home number, and pressed my remote beeper to the receiver to collect my messages. A male voice said I'd left my number on his machine and could call him back at 555-9544. I checked my old black book, which I'd hurriedly stuffed into my purse after Taylor Baines's summons. Angela's number.

I dug another quarter out of my pocket. The man's voice, live this time, identified himself as Roger Price and said he didn't know any Angela. He asked if I'd gotten his number from Together, a local dating service. I asked if he knew Davey Dunrobie. He asked if I wanted to go out for a drink Saturday night. Sunday afternoon would be okay, too, if I was nervous about meeting a strange man at night. He said he was "technically" still married, but eagerly awaiting his divorce decree. I said good-bye.

Then I climbed the stone steps to the library's main entrance, headed to the telephone directories room, and asked for a copy of Cole's numerical. I looked up the untagged phone number from my old black book, the one with the recorded message in the laid-back easy voice, the one who hadn't yet called back, and wrote down the corresponding Charlestown address in my notebook. The street name struck no chimes in my memory. The phone was registered to Joseph P. Jenson. That didn't ring bells either. Back at the pay phone, I tried the number.

The damn answering machine again. I left another plea to get in touch.

I thought about checking out Roz's surveillance gig, decided she and Lemon could probably be relied upon to spot a three-foot-long bright red tube. I crossed Boylston Street to a Pizzeria Uno, sat at the last empty table, and ordered a small pepperoni and anchovy. Then I started making a mental list of the prime live-music bars in the area: Ryles, the Plough, Johnny D's, Harper's Ferry, Midnight the Kats, the Tam, Nightstage — places Dee used to play before she hit big. Joints where somebody might remember Dunrobie, where a sober Dunrobie might look for work.

A lady brought coffee. Abruptly I asked if it was too late to cancel the anchovies. She looked at me a little strangely, but said "no problem" in the heard-it-all voice of a long-term waitress. I left my jacket on my chair so no one would steal the table and headed for the public phone at the back of the restaurant.

Mooney was at his desk. I told him I'd already ordered, and would he like to meet over pizza in the Public Garden?

"No anchovies," he said.

"Not a one."

"Ten minutes."

I sat back down and continued listing music bars on a second paper napkin. By the time the pizza arrived, two matrons toting heavy shopping bags were casting longing looks at my table. I asked the waitress to box the pizza for travel, pack up two soft drinks to go, and bring me the check.

She carried out all requests with dispatch. The pizza smelled crusty and spicy in its cardboard box. I stuffed extra napkins from the take-out counter into my pockets. The shopping-bag matrons descended on my table before I was out the door.

I do better with Mooney if I meet him outside the station. I do a lot better if I bring food.

Mooney is not one of these I've-got-a-secret cops who hoard information for the fun of it. The problem is he expects cooperation. And in the back of my mind I'm always afraid that if I don't keep up with him, favor for favor, he'll want personal attention in return for his help.

He'd probably never pull a stunt like that, but I don't want to risk it. I make an effort to stay ahead on the balance sheet.

We met on the bridge and walked down

the steps to the bench closest to the lagoon. It's a coveted spot on spring days; in today's humid heat, Mooney and I had no competition.

Across the lagoon, a young man was painting one of the swan boats, giving it a needed coat of glistening white. The bird looked ungainly out of the water, its bicycling mechanism indecently exposed. The rest of the fleet floated serenely, laden with tourists waving to nearby camera-pointing family members.

"They have a chance to autopsy the bass player?" I asked, after we'd each devoured a wedge. I always toss the crust to the squirrels. Mooney eats the whole thing.

"No such thing as a free lunch, huh?"

"Just asking."

"It's not a rush job, not with all the gunshots and stabbings. I hear it's gonna be two to a drawer at the morgue pretty soon."

It's been a bad year for Boston homicides. The drug supply starts to dwindle, the big fish eat the little ones.

Mooney chewed a hunk of pizza, took a swig of Pepsi, and said, "Everybody I've talked to says the bass player was 'moody.' Of course, I'm talking to musicians here, music people. I haven't talked to anybody I'd want to certify normal. And moody doesn't mean suicidal."

"Family?"

"Mother called after the local cops came round to break the news. Sounded as okay as anybody could, given the circumstances. Flying in from Topeka, Kansas. The father's dead. Siblings someplace."

"The prescription bottles on the table?"

"You want a whole lot for a little pizza."

"I didn't order anchovies. And maybe I've got something to trade."

"I love maybes."

The swan-boat painter finished the tip of one wing, circled his handiwork admiringly.

Mooney said, "One of the prescriptions belonged to the stiff. Anxiety medication. Serax. Low-grade stuff. The other was written to Dee Willis. Dalmane. Thirty milligrams. Legit scrip. So we know the victim saw a doctor, possibly a shrink, recently. I've got somebody out tracking the doctor. Also the L.A. doc who gave your buddy sleeping pills for the road."

"But — "

"Don't rush me. But there's nothing yet to say that the drugs in the bottle are what the bass player took, right? We have to wait for the tox screen. Now, what have you got for me?"

"Remember we talked about somebody moving the body to Dee's room?"

"I asked a uniform to check at the desk,

but none of the clerks confessed to handing out a duplicate key to 812. Of course, hotel clerks lie to cops in uniform just for practice."

I chewed a disk of pepperoni. The young man across the lagoon was still circling the swan, eyeing it from different angles.

"Did you ask to see all the linen in the hotel last night?" I said. "Or tell the manager to report any heavily soiled sheets or towels or stuff?"

"Damn," he said. "I just checked Brenda's room, not the whole hotel."

"Too late to do the rest now?"

"I'll call when I get back," he said.

"And Brenda's 'boy-toy'?"

"You got something on him, or are we back to my turn?"

"Your turn, Mooney. Have another slice. I'm not that hungry."

"You're always hungry. We can't even pin a name on the boyfriend, other than Ray."

I tossed an edge of crust to a lagoon-swimming duck. Several others appeared from nowhere and converged in V-shaped formation. "Great," I said. "All this case needs is a guy named Ray with no last name."

"You are gonna tell me about the park, right?" Mooney asked.

"You don't think Dee had anything to do with Brenda's death, Moon, do you?"

"I'm supposed to write her off because she's your friend?" he said.

"Based on the evidence," I said evenly.

"Somebody wiped all the prints at the scene. Makes her look like a suspect."

"Maybe her manager and her producer got a little carried away trying to protect her, Mooney. Aren't you guys overdoing it a little?"

"She's Dee Willis. I don't want some city councillor or the mayor getting on my case about how we treat the rich and famous one way and the poor another."

"Is there any heat to arrest her?"

"Not till after the autopsy. Probably not till after the concert. She brings bucks to our fair city."

"Justice for all," I said.

"I'm glad you're asking questions," he said.

"You are?"

"It makes me think you don't know a whole lot more than I do."

I crushed the pizza carton so it would fit in the bag with the empty soft-drink cups.

"You are planning to tell me about the park," Mooney repeated.

I wondered if I should introduce Dunrobie's name. Mooney might be able to find him faster than I could.

"She was looking for an old friend," I said. "A guy we both used to know, come way down in the world."

"Usually those are the friends you don't want to find. They find you."

"Well, Dee wants to find him."

"Romance?"

I pretended to consider it. "Maybe guilt. She made it in the business; he didn't."

"Guilt's funny, huh? A couple of my guys would like to arrest Willis just 'cause she's acting so damned guilty. I mean, why's she running around yelling she should have called the doctor, maybe this Brenda was still alive? That babe — excuse me — that lady had been dead for hours."

"Yeah," I said slowly, "I heard her say that stuff, but she didn't seem like herself, you know, didn't seem connected to what was going on."

"Shock?" he said. "Drugs?"

"No," I said. "More like she thought she was somewhere else, like she was remembering something. . . ."

"Go on," Mooney said.

"This could be total crap, but Dee — Dee and I — had a friend who killed herself. A woman — a girl then — Lorraine Holbrook. Dee was one of the people who discovered her body, I think. I'm not a hundred percent sure on that. But even on the phone, Dee sounded weird, like she was flashing back — "

"Acid?" Mooney said.

"I'm not talking about any drug-induced hallucination. I just mean another death, a similar death, could have thrown her, made her remember that other time."

Lorraine, I thought suddenly. "Sweet Lorraine." A song title. A song.

"How'd you get mixed up with this whole weird crew?" Mooney asked.

"Huh?"

"Not that cops aren't weird. I was just wondering. You okay?"

I kept my face carefully blank. "You mean, how I met Dee? Through the music. Dee and I once played together in a group. We're old guitar friends from a lifetime ago."

"Old guitar friends" didn't say half of it. For me, a kid who'd picked up most of what I knew about the blues off scratchy 78's, watching Dee play was a revelation and an education. If I'd been a novice painter in nineteenth-century Holland, it would have been like having van Gogh, that weird guy down the street, teach me a little about color.

I tried again. "I even thought about turning professional. I don't think I was ever quite good enough, but I was backing Dee, and she makes you sound so damn fine. She studied with the Reverend Gary Davis. You know who that is?"

I expected Mooney's negative nod and went right on. "Just one of the greatest of the great old bluesmen. She was one of his last students; he left her his guitar when he died. Reverend Davis — I saw him play once — the highest praise he ever gave another player, he'd say: 'Right sportin' playin'.' I remember every single time Dee said that to me. Just about gave me chills."

"You sound like you'd be more than willing to do her a favor," Mooney said softly.

"Look, there was a time I'd have given my left leg to be Dee Willis. I admire her, and I love her, and I guess I hate her too. And it plain doesn't matter. She's a music person. Nothing really matters to her but the music."

"But the two of you were real close?"

"Yeah. We were best buddies."

Mooney shifted on the bench, stared at a tuft of brownish grass. "Dee — uh, she ever come on to you?"

"You want to hit me with that again?" I said.

"Look, Carlotta, we found this Brenda woman bare-ass in Dee's bed. I'm not saying — Shit. I'm just asking: She ever come on to you?"

"We used to massage each other's feet. That turn you on?"

"Might of at the time," Mooney said.

"Dee Willis has always had an eye for guys," I said.

He wiped his face with a paper napkin, scrunched it into a ball, and sighed reproachfully. "And you never introduced me."

I said dryly, "I introduced a guy to Willis once."

"Yeah?"

"My ex-husband. That's the last guy I introduced to Dee Willis."

Mooney grinned ear to ear. "I didn't know you cared," he said.

"You ready to go?"

"One more thing. I happened to see a memo on Joanne Triola's desk."

Shit, I thought.

"Why are you asking about Mickey Manganero?"

"I met him at a party," I said truthfully.

"And you're having Triola check him out as a future date?"

"Mooney," I said, "the party was a big free-for-all tossed by Dee's recording company. I wondered what he was doing there, that's all."

"You see him talk to Brenda? To anybody?"

"Yeah. He was talking to me."

"He's a piece of shit," Mooney said.

"That's why I called Triola instead of Boy Scouts of America," I said.

"Ask your boyfriend about him yet?"

"I haven't seen Sam lately."

"Good," Mooney said.

"You'd rather I was dating Dee Willis?"

"Geez," Mooney said. "You're impossible."

CHAPTER TWENTY

"What do you mean, you don't know where the tube went? A yard-long bright red tube? Ouch!" Hot bacon grease spattered my arm as I let the flame get too high under the skillet.

"*Az der moygen iz leydik der moyekh oykh leydik.* When the stomach is empty, so is the brain." That's another one of the Yiddish sayings my grandmother passed along to my mom. It must be true. I certainly felt lightheaded listening to Roz.

"Calm down," Roz murmured. My mother used to say that a lot, too, in Yiddish and in English. Not when I was frying bacon. My mother, rest her soul, would have had heart failure if anybody had tried to cook bacon in her kosher kitchen.

Bacon is one of my favorite foods. Anything unkosher is one of my favorite foods. I sometimes wonder if this indicates unacknowledged hostility toward my mother — or just a good set of taste buds.

Lemon, that wise teacher of the martial arts, said nothing.

"It went in," Roz reported. "Nine forty-two, mailman brought it."

"And?"

"Gone."

"What do you mean, gone?"

"Me and Lemon, we're both looking for a red tube."

"Yeah?"

"So some guy comes out with a big box, a real big brown cardboard box. Like for a TV set or something."

"Oh, no," I said.

"After he drove away, Lemon said something about how the box seemed light, you know, for its size."

"Right," I said, spearing bacon slices with a fork, flipping them over.

"I went up to the secretarial-service place and the tube was gone. Guy picked it up twenty minutes ago."

"Tell me more," I said.

"Stop waving that fork at me!"

I lowered it. "Well?"

"Well, they're a mailing service, right?" Roz said defensively. "First off, they don't want to tell me anything. Then one of the young chicks, maybe a newcomer, says that the guy started out the door with the tube, then turned around and asked if he could buy a carton, something the tube would fit in. He bought their largest size."

"Smart," I said. "Too damned smart."

"Then this frizzy-haired biddy started yelling at the girl, saying, 'We never discuss the clientele.' I got bounced."

I said, "And he just drove away?"

"Pickup truck." Roz stared at the dirty linoleum. "And we didn't get the license. We weren't interested in a guy moving a TV set."

"You sure it was a guy?"

"Uh, not a hundred percent."

"What did he or she look like?"

"He wore a cap. I only saw his back. Thin. Sneakers. I'm pretty sure it was a man, but I couldn't swear to it."

"Limp?"

"Huh?"

"Did the guy, the girl, whatever, limp? Walk funny?"

Roz looked at Lemon. He stared back at her. "I, uh, don't think so," Roz said faintly.

"Damn." I lowered the flame, broke two eggs directly into the pan, fished out a sliver of shell with a fingertip. My mother used to break each egg separately in a small glass dish, so that if any shell got in the egg or, God-forbid, a rotten or blood-blemished egg appeared, she wouldn't have to start over again.

I'd been hoping Dunrobie would stroll unthinkingly into the trap and make my list of music bars — my proposed evening's entertainment — unnecessary.

"I'm real sorry." Lemon finally said something, shrugging his sloping shoulders. "I won't even charge you for the time. And believe me, business is bad."

Lemon's "business," besides free-lance karate lessons, involves juggling and passing a hat in Harvard Square. The pass-a-hat line has never been lucrative.

"Going out tonight?" I asked Roz.

"Yeah."

"Good." It would have been a shame to waste her outfit on me. She was wearing a Day-Glo lime-green T-shirt that proclaimed: "Sailors get blown offshore." To complement it, she'd chosen hot-pink spandex tights and orange hightop sneakers. The ensemble went well with her skunk-striped hair.

"Yeah."

"The Rat?" I inquired, naming one of her favorite Kenmore Square dives, where groups with names like "Slimeball Slugs on Meth" play to audiences dressed in dog chains.

"The Rat, the Roxy, a couple others."

I said, "Can you ask around for a guitar player named Davey. Six feet, white, skinny. Heavy drinker. Druggie. If you get a hit, see if they know his last name."

"Which is?"

"Dunrobie. Don't spread it around."

"So then I'll be working for you tonight?"

I raised an incredulous eyebrow. "You want me to pay you?" I couldn't blame her for asking. The only way I'd go to those places is if somebody else paid. "Forget it," I said.

"Hey," she said. "Worth a try. Don't worry. I'll ask about the guy. To make up for today, okay?"

I carefully slid the eggs out of the pan, breaking both.

And I forgot to ask about the locks.

CHAPTER TWENTY-ONE

I changed clothes several times before deciding on the appropriate attire for a bar crawl. I wanted to look approachable, but not eager. Above all, I did not want to look like a working woman, and prostitutes are hard to peg, since they don't constrain themselves to TV producers' ideas of what they ought to wear.

Unaccompanied men can walk into bars without raising many eyebrows, but you need a bit of protective coloring to fit in as a lone woman. A waitress's outfit would be ideal. Or a nun's habit, the old-fashioned full-dress version, complete with wimple.

Lacking such body armor, the best way to avoid trouble is to arrive with an escort. I considered my choices. Mooney would be delighted, if he wasn't working. But Mooney looks too much like what he is, and his presence often gives the most willing gossip a temporary case of lockjaw. My other option was Sam Gianelli.

I met Gianelli when I first drove a cab for Green & White, back in college. He hired me, and taught me many things, like never sleep with your boss. I'm descended from cops; he's descended from robbers, his dad being a local Mafia underboss. The only thing we have in common is that old boy-girl stuff I never understand. There are probably a thousand guys who'd be better for me than Sam Gianelli.

What I could use right now is a twenty-year-old bimbo-lifeguard type, unmarriageable and unchallenging. Restful.

What Sam needs is a submissive Italian Catholic virgin, certified fertile, so Papa Gianelli can have a pack of grandkids.

We've both been married before. After Cal, I retired; never again. Sam, on the other hand, just got back from Italy, where he visited the old-country side of the family. One of the items on his agenda turned out to be a surprise trip to the Vatican to petition for an annulment. Papa arranged it; he believes in marriage even more than Sam does.

Half-Jewish divorcée that I am, if I *did* want to marry Sam, his father would probably have me garroted, shot for good measure, and dropped into Boston Harbor.

I decided to go alone. I called a cab. Cheaper than a traffic ticket or a parking lot.

Midnight the Kat's was the fourth bar I hit, after Harper's Ferry, Ryles, and Dixie's. I'd started out on beer and was still sober because

183

I'd long since switched to club soda with a twist of lime, a drink that can pass for a vodka-and-tonic anyday.

Midnight's is near Auditorium Station. I remember when it was called the Vanity, which dates me, but I got into the blues scene young. The Vanity's where I heard the Reverend Gary Davis, the awesome blues preacher himself, play. He was an old man then. Dee got me the tickets. She was studying with him, five bucks a lesson, paid up front, and the lesson could last all day if the teacher stayed pleased with his pupil.

Midnight's is half bar, half performance-hall. You walk into the bar first, heavy with cigarette smoke, then descend three steps to the music room with its pine-board floor and rickety tables.

The sign over the door says the fire department allows fifty-five patrons. I've never counted, but I think the management must pay somebody off, weekends at least. You don't get the superstars at a small place like this, not even the second rank. People on the way up, or the way down. Some are pretty damn good, and often the best seem on the slide rather than on the make.

I shrugged out of my raincoat for the fourth time. I'd decided to dress down, as usual. Most of my shoes have flat heels, since at six one

I don't need to emphasize my height. In good beige slacks and a turquoise shirt, with a tapestry vest, and a gold chain around my neck, I looked, to my eye at least, like a stock analyst, or a lawyer. Somebody who'd arrived early and was waiting for the rest of the group.

I eyed my watch conspicuously to go with my cover story, comparing it with the wall clock. Ten minutes to twelve. Then, with a sigh, I took a seat at the bar. I ordered my club soda from a man with hairy arms and an anchor tattoo. The TV was tuned to the Red Sox game, which was still in rain delay. The umps would call it at one if the rain didn't quit by then. The sportscasters were drowned out by music, somebody's mushy version of "Kind Woman." The control panel for the stage amps was behind the bar along with the rest of the sound system. Lights flashed as the volume of the music rose and fell.

The stage was an irregularly shaped platform in the far corner of the music room, lit by three baby spots fastened to a low-slung horizontal iron pipe. Loops of cable wrapped the pipe and disappeared into the false ceiling.

I asked the hairy-armed barkeep who was playing tonight. He made a show of staring at a sign posted behind the bar, a calendar with print so small he had to squint.

"Windshear," he said. "New group. First

set coming up. Start in maybe fifteen, twenty minutes."

I sipped and crowd-watched until a young man came out and fiddled with the microphones, making sure all the cables were plugged into the right jacks, checking the amps on either side of the stage.

He had long pony-tailed hair, black jeans, and a faded black T-shirt. He looked familiar, but that was because I'd talked to somebody just like him at the past four bars.

The crowd had changed from the office escapees of the earlier hours. They were younger, dressed more for display than the muggy August night. There were a couple of serious drinkers at the bar, maybe businessmen far from home, nobody who looked smashed. A few regulars called the bartender Artie.

The pony-tailed man brought out a guitar and placed it on a stand, stage left.

I got up and checked out the brand name.

"Hey," he said, "careful."

"That a DeArmond pickup?" I asked, taking a step away from the guitar, which was a nice old Gibson SJN, electrified for the occasion.

"Yeah," the guy said.

"Yours?"

"I wish."

"You with the band or the house?"

"The band," he said, starting to preen a little. "I'm the boards. I play synth, mini-Moog, the whole thing."

"I'm guitar."

"Play local?"

"Yeah. Some."

"Got an ax as nice as that one?"

"Pretty good," I said.

We traded brand names and who-do-you-knows until I'd established my bona fides. I asked him if he'd heard Chris Smither play at Johnny D's, and when the last time the Zydeco band had been through, and then I asked him if he knew a Davey who played a big old whanging Gibson Hummingbird.

If Davey had kept anything from his pre-alcoholic life, that would be it. He loved that guitar.

Maybe I'd have to try pawnshops, used instrument shops. . . .

"Hey," the guy said, "this a joke?"

"No."

"I know a guy plays a Hummingbird, but he ain't no Davey."

"Who?" I said.

"Plays bass mainly," he said. "Cal. Some kind of Cajun last name. He's with the band."

CHAPTER TWENTY-TWO

I ordered a quick double bourbon from the hairy bartender and carried it to the most inconspicuous table I could find. I slid one of the two chairs over to a table for six, hoping they could seat seven and I could have privacy. Plunk your butt at a table with an empty chair, guys tend to come over to chat. It's almost a formal invitation.

I took a gulp of whiskey. I wanted to be alone when the lights dimmed, and not entirely sober.

If he'd had plastic surgery I'd have known him. I could watch those hands on that bass, just the hands, and know them.

The startling thing was how little he'd changed. His hair was short, his beard gone. Why had he kept the mustache? I wondered irrelevantly.

Why had I assumed I'd know if he were back in town? Why had I assumed Dee would know, would tell me? "He left a long time ago," she had said; that's all. I'd made up the rest, embroidered my own acceptable tale:

he'd walked out on tour, settled on the West Coast. Why had I placed him in California? Maybe he'd mentioned it once or twice, wanting to go to Los Angeles, play studio stuff, bask in the sunshine.

I ordered another drink from a waitress with waist-length brown hair. It took me a while to get her attention. She was scouting the band, eyeing Cal. I'd never gotten over that in the short time we'd been married, the way women would watch him, the way I was watching him now.

He wore a black short-sleeved T-shirt, tight enough to show muscle and rib. I checked his arms carefully. He never wore short sleeves near the end, not after he'd started shooting cocaine. He still held his left arm oddly, awkwardly, to give his thumb more reach, he always said, more strength on the frets. During his first solo break, the spotlight picked up the mother-of-pearl inlay work on his bass. It was the same bass he'd always had. I was surprised he hadn't hocked it to pay for dope.

He could have been playing alone in the bedroom. That's the way he always played, like he was the only one alive on a desert island, just him and the song. His eyes were half open, but they might as well have been blind. He didn't see the waitress. He didn't see me. He was just there in the music.

I sat through three long sets. The lead guitar, a guy with a kerchief headband and a reedy tenor, was too gimmicky by half, in love with his technology. He leaned on the whammy pedal, distorting all over the place, bending notes that didn't ask to be bent. He was the kind of guitar player who wants to show off his sixty-fourth notes when sixteenths would suit the song.

Windshear didn't impress me; they didn't seem to have a sound yet, just four players: guitar, bass, boards, and drums. No lightning sparked. They did steady twelve-bar blues, a little classic rock and roll.

Nothing caught fire until Cal's last solo break, and I wasn't sure if the heat transferred to the rest of the audience or if it started and stopped with me, rising slowly from my toes to my cheeks. I've long since given up on Prince Charming, but if mine ever comes calling, he's not going to tote a glass slipper or ride a white steed. He'll play bass like Cal Therieux. Sing close harmony in a grumbly baritone, always right on key.

Trying to wrench my mind back to business, I wondered when Cal had bought Davey's old Hummingbird.

No way to tell unless I asked.

CHAPTER TWENTY-THREE

Near the end of the final set I found myself wondering what Miss Manners would advise about consulting an ex-husband on a business matter.

Probably to avoid watching him in concert if his bass playing still turns you on. I tried not to watch Cal's hands, which was impossible.

When the encore ended to scattered applause, the stragglers shuffled through a haze of cigarette smoke, hesitated at the doorway, yanking out umbrellas. I listened to the rain pelt the sidewalk. The waitress yawned as she bused my table.

Cal was arguing with the lead guitar. He reached over and plucked the man's A string, grimaced at the flat twang. The pony-tailed keyboard player gave me a glance when I stood, and murmured something to Cal, who turned to look at me, shading his eyes from the spotlight glare.

"Carly?"

Nobody calls me Carly. Nobody ever did except Cal.

"Hi," I said, expelling a deep breath.

There was a pause. He hadn't read Miss Manners on chatting with ex-spouses either.

"So how are you?" he said finally, taking twice as long as necessary to unhook his bass strap. It was intricately tooled leather. I'd given him that strap.

"Okay." I walked up the two steps to the stage, taking extra care not to trip over a cable. "You?"

"Okay."

Another pause. Cal tucked his bass into a hardshell case.

"Can I buy you a drink?" I asked.

"No."

"Just no?" I asked.

"Not here," he said. "They lock up so fast, sometimes I get my foot caught in the door." Then he lowered his voice so the curious keyboard player couldn't overhear. "Not anyplace."

Stung, I said, "Last time I saw you, you wouldn't turn down a drink."

"Yeah, well, I'm clean and sober now," he said. "Stone-cold. Two years, two months."

"Good for you," I said, meaning it. "Look, I don't care about the drink. I want to talk."

"Not here. And not at my place."

I wondered if he was living with somebody, married even.

"You have an unlisted number."

"I don't have a phone," he said.

"I wish I'd known you were in town. Would have made my life easier," I said.

"Yeah, but that's not my job, is it?"

Two waiters piled chairs on top of tables. The waitress swept underneath as fast as they stacked them. The barkeep checked the clock.

There aren't too many joints to hit in Boston at two in the morning. It's not New Orleans.

"Maybe we could take a walk," I said.

"Okay."

I'm a late-night walker. Rain doesn't deter me. A downpour does. The wind scooped water off the sidewalk and dumped it into my shoes, turned my umbrella into a useless sail. Cal, with no umbrella or raincoat, zipped up his denim jacket and stuck the hand that wasn't holding the bass into his pocket.

"Do you know any place that's open?" I hollered into the gale. "A doughnut shop? A diner? All the after-hours places I know are cop hangouts."

"It's your call," Cal said impassively, rain dripping off his chin.

I always try to flag a Green & White out of company loyalty, but this time I grabbed the first available cab, a Yellow, piloted by a Haitian who crept along at half speed.

Cal, sharing the backseat, his knees straddling his bass, seemed like a stranger; everything I remembered about our marriage seemed like something I'd read in a book, like it had happened to somebody else.

I gave the cabbie my address.

"How'd you get clean?" I asked.

"AA."

"I thought you had to believe in God for AA."

"A Higher Power. Bothered me some at the beginning, but it turned into an easy choice: believe in something, or wind up dead in some stinking hole with a needle in your arm. AIDS scared the hell out of me. I always thought I'd die young, but that's sure not the way I want to go."

"Motorcycle crash," I suggested with a lifted eyebrow.

"Yeah," he said. "Blast of glory. James Dean. Dick Fariña. Instead I go to AA."

"Good for you," I repeated.

"And I play bass with whoever pays," he said.

We didn't talk during the rest of the ride. The windshield wipers slapped out a squishy rhythm. I paid the fare.

I'd stuck my duplicate keys into my back pocket. My hair was drenched by the time I got all the locks open.

"Yeah," Cal said, dripping on the foyer rug.

"I remember this. Nice place. Big."

I stuck my umbrella in the stand, stepped out of my soaked shoes.

"Okay if I take my shoes off?" Cal asked.

"Yeah," I said.

"Can I leave the bass here? Case is wet."

"Just leave it," I said. "I'll get towels. Be right back."

"Your aunt would have yelled a blue streak, water all over her floor."

"Yeah, well, I'm not her."

I raced upstairs to the linen closet, yanked out two turquoise towels. I bent at the waist to secure one of them around my head, turban style, and headed toward the bathroom.

It was the first thing I saw when I stepped through the door. Across the mirror, someone had printed the words crookedly: "Back off" in blood red. Lipstick, I realized. The floor was littered with broken medicine bottles, assorted tablets. Cough medicine trickled across the tile.

I ran downstairs.

"You always looked good in towels, Carly," Cal said.

I pushed past him into the living room. The sofa was upended; its weak leg finally split. Cal must have followed. I heard him gasp.

"Call 911," I said.

"Somebody might still be here."

"Call 911," I repeated.

"What the hell are you gonna do with that thing?"

While he was dialing, I'd opened the lower-left-hand drawer of my desk, quickly unwrapping my .38 from its undershirt shroud.

"I had to make sure it wasn't stolen," I snapped.

"Is anything gone?" he asked.

I turned in a slow circle, the .38 pointing at the floor. Aunt Bea's mahogany end tables had been smashed. The Oriental rug looked like it had sprouted a new pattern. From the emptied food jars nearby — peanut butter, mustard, ketchup — I could guess the artist's medium. The room smelled; he'd used worse. Urine. Feces, maybe.

"T.C.!" I called, while Cal was giving my address to the Cambridge police.

I took off upstairs, gripping the gun. There aren't a lot of things I care about in that house. T.C., my cat, is one of them. It's odd that I thought about him before Roz. Maybe not. Roz, with her karate training, can look after herself. And Roz was the one who was supposed to have had the damned locks changed.

I did a room-by-room search, aware that it ought to be left to the cops, aware that I was taking reckless chances. I felt like taking reckless chances. I felt like catching whoever had smashed Aunt Bea's carefully polished end tables into splinters, turned her prized rug into a spoiled canvas — catching him and hurting him.

Not killing him. Hurting him. Badly.

I heard a noise on the staircase, pivoted. "Carly, they're on their way."

"Ten minutes, right?" They always say that.

"Can you do me a favor?"

"What?"

"Put the gun down."

"You do me one too."

"Yeah?"

"Call me Carlotta."

"You got the gun, I call you whatever you want."

I lowered it to my side, feeling angry and foolish. "Damn," I said. "Dammit to hell."

T.C. burst out of the linen closet and scooted to my side. He didn't even yowl and scratch when I picked him up.

"Come downstairs," Cal said. "I'll buy you a drink."

CHAPTER TWENTY-FOUR

The cops took twenty minutes to arrive. There were two of them, what they call a salt-and-pepper team, one black, one white. They could have called this team a Laurel-and-Hardy. The white man was so fat, I didn't see how he'd passed the physical, unless they'd weighed him with his skinny partner and divided by two. They made Cal and me wait outside in the rain while they did the same room-by-room search I'd done, guns drawn. They came downstairs chuckling like it was the most fun they'd had all night.

Then, their muddy footprints all over the place, they invited us back into my living room. The fat one pulled out a form and handed it to the skinny one, who started filling it out.

I hadn't expected anything else. It was late. Routine housebreak was what these guys expected to see. My neighborhood is popular with burglars.

"Aren't you gonna dust for fingerprints?" Cal demanded. "Take photographs? You see that mirror in the bathroom? She's been threatened, for chrissake!"

"Witnesses?" the fat cop said evenly, looking straight at Cal.

"The cat," I said. "Hid in a closet." The wallop of a hurriedly downed Scotch was starting to catch up with the earlier double bourbon and the long-ago beer.

"Boyfriend? Husband?" the thin black cop said, nodding at Cal.

"Yeah," Cal said defensively. "Ex."

"You have anything to do with this?" the fat cop asked.

"No, as a matter of fact, I didn't."

"Some guys do, have it arranged. Prove to the little woman she can't hack it living alone."

"That the kind of help you give, nickel psychology?" Cal asked.

"You piss anybody off lately?" the black cop asked me. "Fire anybody? Give somebody the finger?"

"Me?" I said innocently. "The little woman?"

"It was kids," the fat cop said, smoothing it over. "Do it all the time. Probably saw the lipstick-writing thing on TV. Miracle they spelled two words right. Peanut butter and jelly on the rug. Shit, too, unless that's from the cat. Kids got no respect for property."

"Broken glass," the black cop observed,

shaking his head, and scuffing around the living room. "Probably sent a brick through your window and climbed in. Good locks. Couldn't force 'em. Oughta get these windows boarded up tonight. Know an all-night place?"

"Yeah," I said, wondering if either of the cops would notice anything odd about the pattern of breakage.

"Your insurance probably covers glass," the white guy said. "Take photos."

"I will," I said. Suddenly I just wanted them out of my house. I needed time to think. "Good night. Thanks for coming so quickly," I said.

Cal stared at me like I needed a quick brain scan.

"Sorry this had to happen," the black cop said. "You write out a list of stolen items and get it into the station. Xerox a copy for your insurance company."

I made some remark about the lousy weather, and all the creeps coming out on a night like this.

Long as it killed the heat, they said, they didn't mind. Then they sped on their way.

"What's going on, Carly?" Cal said, trying to stare me down.

"Carlotta," I reminded him absently. "Look, why don't you go home? We can talk tomorrow."

"I'm too wired to go home. I'll help pick up the glass."

"Yeah," I said. "The glass."

"What's that mean?"

"You see much glass in this room?"

"No."

"That's because the windows were broken from the inside."

"The inside?" Cal repeated.

"Yeah," I said. " 'But then how did the little pranksters get in?' asked the cops."

"They didn't ask."

"Yeah, but if they had, I could have told them."

"Tell me."

"They used my keys."

"Maybe you should call the cops back," Cal said after a long pause.

"Maybe you should go home," I said.

"Maybe you should call that all-night glass-repair place."

I'd lied to the cops. I don't know an all-night window-boarder. I do know Gloria, the dispatcher at G&W. And Gloria has three brothers, the smallest of whom got booted out of the NFL for playing too rough. They do odd jobs at odd hours. I never inquire too deeply into their current employment.

One SOS to Gloria, and they were available. They boarded the front windows with half-inch plywood, cursed the filthy weather, and told me somebody would be by with glass in the morning.

I treated them to the remainder of Roz's bottle of Scotch. I figured she owed it to me for not getting the locks changed fast enough. While the brothers hammered, Cal helped me take inventory and clean. Not that there was much we could do. The rug needed professional care. We figured we'd do more harm than good, tackling it with home remedies, so we rolled it up, filth and all, and stood it on end in the hallway.

I fed the cat. His cans of FancyFeast had been left untouched, and it made me feel better to see him hunker down, a calm oasis, in his special corner.

A five-pound sack of flour had been dumped in the middle of the kitchen floor. The assailant — I thought of him that way, as the assailant — had then emptied two cans of pie cherries and a big plastic bottle of maple syrup over the pile. Then he'd swept a broom through it, making sure the goo spread before hardening.

In the living room, Cal's denim jacket hung from the coat tree, his wet socks from the cold radiator. He'd put his shoes back on because of the broken glass. He'd righted the couch. He wore the turquoise towel draped around his shoulders like a fighter; his hair was wet and spiky from rain or sweat. He held my silver-framed photo of Paolina in his big hands, picking shards of glass away from the print, and turned to me with a question in his eyes.

"My little sister," I said.

"I thought she might be your kid."

"From the Big Sisters Organization."

He set the photo down, ran a careful hand over the wooden mantel. "You're not married?" he asked.

"No. You?" I returned.

"No."

He started filling another trash bag with debris. I remembered him after performances — on a natural high, adrenaline-pumped. That's why he drank, he'd tell me. That's why he doped. He had to come down, had to come down from the performing high. He was too wired to sleep, but so tired, so tired.

"This happen to you often?" he asked.

"No."

"And I thought I had a crummy job," he said.

"Sit down," I said.

"No. No, this works. Maybe I should get a job cleaning buildings nights, after playing with that crummy band. Group's been together barely a month, and already it feels wrong. Roger, the lead guitar, he couldn't front a washboard trio."

I was reluctant to sit while he paced, so I picked up the remains of a kitchen mug and tossed it into a doubled Hefty Bag. At least nobody had slit the upholstery. But then, why should they? Nobody was trying to find anything here. They were just trying to warn me off.

Warn me off what?

"You had a good solo in the third set," I said to Cal, grateful for his help and his company. Roz hadn't returned from her pub crawl yet. Maybe she wouldn't. Not till long past daybreak. "Second from the last song."

"Yeah," he said. "One decent break, the whole night."

"You could find a better band," I said.

"Oh, sure. People waiting in line for ex-addict bass players," he said. "Standing in line. You play much?"

"Just practice," I said.

"You still got your National?"

"Under my bed," I said. I wished I hadn't mentioned the word "bed." It sounded louder in my ears than it should have.

"I'll play you a song," he said, too casually.

"This is business, Cal. This whole mess, this break-in, has something to do with a case I'm working on."

"Does that mean it might have something

to do with me?"

"You might be able to help me."

"Why would I?"

"For auld acquaintance," I said.

He squatted, dumped pieces of broken china into a bag. "You remember sneaking around in here while your aunt was alive? Before we got married? She knew what we were up to, old Bea. She wasn't so dumb."

"Yeah," I said. "I knew she knew, and she knew I knew she knew, but we needed to keep up the front, you know? Some kind of generational thing."

He stood up. "You got any older generations in the house?"

"No."

"So, you wanna dance?" He turned to me abruptly, threw out the words like a challenge.

They were the first words he ever said to me, the day after my nineteenth birthday. We were at a concert. Nobody was dancing. There wasn't even a dance floor.

In our lovers' language, "Wanna dance" became shorthand for something far more intimate.

"In the middle of this?"

"Nobody got hurt, not even the cat. We should celebrate."

"I imagine you've done a lot of dancing since me," I said.

"I imagine you have too. I'm healthy," he said. "Checked and inspected."

"Me too," I said. "Healthy."

"I use condoms, if requested."

"Is there somebody at home waiting for you, Cal?"

"Just the rats and the roaches."

"No woman who's gonna hate us both in the morning?"

"Nope."

"Promise?"

He touched my cheek with callused fingertips and the shock wave traveled to the nape of my neck and exploded.

"I need to find Davey Dunrobie," I said.

"Tonight?" he asked softly, his mouth a quarter of an inch from mine. "Right now?"

"No."

CHAPTER
TWENTY-FIVE

I woke slowly, wondering why I felt so hot. On a steamy August night I wouldn't wear so much as a T-shirt to bed, much less drape myself with my quilt. Half asleep, I tried to shove the heavy weight aside.

Ah. I stopped mid-push. Not a quilt. A man . . .

Last night's liquor furred my tongue. Hot summer nights, Sam and I sleep in his Charles River Park apartment in air-conditioned bliss.

Not Sam. Cal, my ex-husband.

Cal, my ex-husband, stirred and moaned, rolled over onto the pillow beside me. I stretched cautiously. Aside from my tongue, I discovered that the rest of me felt great.

"Never sleep with your ex-husband."

I comforted myself with the thought that my grandmother would never have dreamed of such a situation, and therefore couldn't possibly have passed on a relevant Yiddish saying to my mom.

My vest dangled from the back of a chair. My panties were snagged on the handle of the bedside table drawer. The rest of our clothes littered the floor. I couldn't see my shoes.

The rain. Wet shoes in the hall. No. We'd put our shoes back on because of the glass.

The glass! I sat up quickly. What the hell time was it? Would a truckload of glaziers be arriving momentarily?

Cal groaned softly and yanked at the sheet. I touched his arm. His narrow-shouldered body had aged well; he was leaner, harder. Last night my exploring hand had touched a scar near his flat stomach.

Appendectomy or barroom brawl. I'd have to ask.

I eased out of bed naked, crossed to the phone, dialed hurriedly. I spoke softly, but I was pretty sure I didn't have to bother with the precaution. The Cal of old could sleep through a thunderstorm.

"Mooney?" I was in luck; he answered on the second ring.

"Yeah?"

"Don't you ever go home?"

"Why this sudden interest in my personal life?"

I shifted gears fast. "Anything on the bass player's autopsy?" If the cops were satisfied with suicide, I figured there was no need to stir things up, busted windows or no.

"Doesn't look great for your friend."

"What does that mean?"

I could hear him shuffling papers. "Let me translate from the patholog-ese," he muttered. "Here it is. Looks like our female Caucasian — Hunter, Brenda Alice, Miss — got a three-way hit: booze, pills, and just to make sure, an injection. Speedball-type thing, cocaine and heroin. And the kicker is that we found no works — no needle, no syringe. So what we got is this: We got her in Dee Willis's bed, dead meat. And we got Dee Willis, first on the scene, and a bunch of hangers-on lying to keep her from incriminating herself. It may have been an accident, but, hell, she probably killed the girl. What did they give the girl who shot up John Belushi? Second degree?"

"That woman had the works on her and a drug rap-sheet as long as my arm, Mooney. She admitted the whole deal. You find a needle in Dee's guitar case?"

"She had plenty of time to ditch it."

I sat on the dresser, resting my toes on the wooden floor. "Mooney, listen. Somebody broke into my house last night."

I moved the phone away from my ear, preparing myself for the explosion. Mooney doesn't think women should live alone. When his dad died, Mom promptly sold the family digs in Southie, and moved in with her darling boy. Mooney rumbled, spluttered, and finally decided not to voice his opinion, bless him. He said "You okay?" in such a mild tone I almost missed it. I was staring at my bed, at Cal's bony foot sticking out from under the sheet.

"I'm fine." I pressed the receiver to my ear and tried to keep a smile out of my voice. "The only reason I'm telling you is, it wasn't any casual kick-in-the-door job. My bag was lifted at the Berklee. Somebody used my keys to get in and trash the place."

"You report the handbag theft?"

"Not exactly. I called Joanne Triola, asked her to let me know if my wallet turned up in a Dumpster. I wasn't carrying more than ten bucks."

"I can't believe you didn't change the locks."

"Roz was supposed to take care of it. And don't say you can't believe I trusted Roz. I can't believe I trusted Roz. Next time I see her, I'm gonna grab her and dye her hair that nasty old-lady blue — after I pull some of it out."

"You're damn lucky you weren't home."

"Somebody left a message on my mirror: Back off."

"Polite," Mooney said. "Usually they write dirty words. And you think it has to do with this Willis business?"

"I don't know what else I'm supposed to back off of."

"I'll come by."

"No," I said hurriedly.

"That Gianelli guy with you?"

I should never phone Mooney when I'm naked. Sometimes I swear he can see over the line. "No," I said truthfully.

"Then I'll come over."

"Mooney, don't waste your time. Use your best skip-trace artist to see if you can find a guy named David Dunrobie." I spelled it for him. "He's the old friend Dee was searching for in the park. Then see if you can pull an old file — and this might be tough, if not impossible. A suicide or accidental. Overdose. The friend I told you about. In 1978 — yeah, don't yell. I know, but I can't help it. October 28, 1978. Lorraine Holbrook."

"Sweet Lorraine." I was almost sure that was one of the song titles from the lawyer's letter, that Davey had claimed Dee's famous "For Tonight" was really his song, "Sweet Lorraine."

"Lived in Jamaica Plain," I said to Mooney.

"Street address?"

"Addison? Maybe Addison Court or Lane."

"Maybe?" Mooney said.

"Sounds right. Look, Mooney, back then, with a presumed suicide — booze and pills

— you think they'd have checked for a possible injection site?"

"In '78? Not unless they thought your lady was shooting heroin. Speedballs only got fashionable since Belushi kicked. Now all the hotshot M.E.'s run a check."

"You got pressure to bust Dee? Make headlines?"

"Nothing I can't handle. But let me get this straight. You think Willis might have killed both these women. Same way?"

"No, Moon, that's not what I think."

"Well, what do you think?"

"Don't get hostile. I think it would be interesting to find out, that's all. Bye now."

Cal's eyes were open when I sat down on the bed.

"Eavesdropping?" I asked.

"I stare at naked ladies too."

I plugged a Rory Block tape into my cassette deck, adjusted the volume, and wriggled in close to him. "That all you do with them?" I asked, batting my eyelashes.

It made us both laugh. He reached for me.

Block sang, "Send the Man Back Home," and we made love again — better than last night, if not as frenzied. Cal seemed to have learned a few new moves since me.

I made sure he used a condom. Hell, I thought, if you can't trust the louse who walked out on you ten years ago, who can you trust?

I got on top to control speed and depth. His callused fingers touched my breasts. I wondered if he found this morning's lovemaking more enjoyable, less like combat. Last night's had left me wondering when he'd last had a woman.

Afterward, I fluttered the top sheet over our sweaty bodies like a giant fan. Propped on one elbow, he rubbed the bridge of my thrice-broken nose with his index finger. "So why didn't you get married again?" he asked. I closed my eyes and forgot about the glaziers and the clock and the mess downstairs.

" 'Cause I'm no fun in bed," I said.

"Fooled me, all that screaming and wiggling."

I listened to Block soar a cappella through the end of "Foreign Lander."

> "I've conquered all my enemies,
> From land and o'er the sea.
> "But you, my dearest new love,
> Your beauty has conquered me."

Cal said, "Good sound system in here."

"Surprised?"

"No."

I couldn't leave his earlier question alone.

"So why haven't I remarried? Number one: you. You soured me on the institution, as if my mom and dad hadn't already done their best. Number two: I hate to compromise." I caught a glimpse of my guitar case lying open on the floor. "Three: I seem to remember you playing me a song last night."

"You must have been drunk."

"Come on. What did you play?"

"Make Me a Pallet on Your Floor," he admitted sheepishly. "Seemed appropriate at the time. Don't get up yet."

"It's late," I said.

"We'll shower together. I'll scrub your back."

He sang to me in the tub while I tried to hurry up, and he tried to slow me down. We attempted "Make Me a Pallet" in ragged harmony, then Cal scat-sang a bass line while I held the melody and he soaped my shoulders.

"Don't you ever turn a stranger from
your door,
Don't you ever turn a stranger from
your door,
For the day may come you'll be a
stranger too,
Just looking for a pallet on the floor."

"I'm supposed to be working," I said firmly,

when Cal's hands started sliding their way around to my breasts.

"Give yourself a break, Carly. Me, too. Relax." He snuggled in closer, pressing his lips to my neck.

I took a deep breath. "Working," I repeated. "Now."

"Okay, lady," he said. "Rinse cycle."

I yanked open the shower curtain and got out first.

Cal towel-dried his hair, watched me fasten my bra in the steamy mirror. "You sleep with everybody you want answers from?"

"Sure," I said with no inflection in my voice. "And they always tell me the absolute truth."

"What absolute truths do I know?"

"Start with Davey Dunrobie," I said.

"You slept with him. I know that for an absolute truth. He told me."

I said, "You slept with Dee Willis. Christ, you slept with every woman who ever admired the way you play."

He backed off and said, "What's going on with Davey?"

"No. You tell me what's going on with Davey."

"We tried AA together, but it didn't stick to him. So I cooled it. It's one of the rules. You can't stay clean when you're hanging with junkies."

"Last time you saw him?"

"Hell, years ago. Three years at least."

"Living where?"

"Some kind of communal thing. Mission Hill."

"Religion?" There are a lot of cult houses in that part of town.

"Vegetarianism and alcohol. Playing reggae."

"Remember any names?"

"Sorry. Maybe something'll come. Malcolm somebody."

"Did Davey ever write songs? When he was playing with Dee?"

"Why?"

I didn't feel like telling him, so I switched the subject. "Why did you leave Dee?"

"I thought you were asking about Davey."

"Why?"

He stuck his wallet into his back pocket. "I didn't leave. I got fired."

I studied his face in the mirror.

"Too doped and too drunk to know when I had it good," he went on. "And I don't mean Dee. By that time we weren't sleeping together. Carly, you know, I kick myself every day for pissing away that music. Dee — whatever it is, whatever it takes to front a band — she's got it. She lets you out, gives you plenty of room to breathe, and then reels you back in like a fish on a line. She works free, but she's grounded. She's just — she's *home* in the blues. She knows where the music starts, and where it ends."

I didn't think I'd ever heard Cal string so many words together. I wondered if he knew Dee would be needing a bass player.

"You're giving me that cop look," he said. "I remember that look."

I said, "Tell me about this Malcolm Somebody."

"Guru type on the Hill. I could find where he lived. We had some parties there, outrageous parties. On second thought, maybe I couldn't find it. Maybe I'd have to get stoned to find it."

"Let's give it a try," I said. "Now. With you sober."

"Carly," he said. "Am I good sober?"

"Good at what?"

"What I do."

"Play bass or make love?"

"Yeah," he said.

"You hold back, Cal," I said, turning to face the mirror and brushing my hair hard. "From everything but the music. How come you need to ask?"

CHAPTER TWENTY-SIX

Downstairs, the window men had arrived, and Lemon was helping them hold panes in place with huge suction cups. Roz, looking as contrite as I've ever seen her, was scrubbing the kitchen floor with what looked like an assortment of paint scrapers. A mop and bucket stood in a corner. Her skunk-striped hair was wound in a turban.

"I'm just gonna stay on my knees," she said. "I forgot about the locks. I'm sorry."

I hate it when people apologize before I get a chance to yell at them.

"Hi," Roz said to Cal, deftly changing the subject. "Do I know you?"

"I'm the ex-husband," Cal said.

Roz's eyebrows shot halfway up her forehead, but she didn't say a word.

Tiptoeing through the glop, I opened the refrigerator. Cal followed me, stared critically at the shelves, and eagerly agreed when I suggested we grab a bite on the way to Mission Hill.

Charlie's Kitchen in Harvard Square does

good fried eggs, but Cal and I used to share them a long time ago, and I didn't want any memories on the side. We bought Egg McMuffins in a bag at the drive-thru McDonald's near Fenway Park. Not much to wax nostalgic about, but quick.

Mission Hill is an integrated zone in color-divided Boston. White residents tend to say they live near the Brigham, short for Brigham and Women's Hospital, the monolith created when Women's Lying-In merged with Peter Bent Brigham Hospital. Black residents say they live on the Hill. For a while the city tried calling it the Parker Hill/Fenway neighborhood in an attempt to improve its tone. Tucked between Boston and Brookline, with Roxbury its closest neighbor, the Hill has a bad reputation. I make sure my cab doors are locked before I take a night fare to the Hill.

"You drive yet?" I asked Cal as we made our way slowly up Huntington Avenue, dodging the trolley tracks.

"I learned, but I don't have a car."

"Automatic or stick?"

"Automatic."

I don't really consider that anybody who only drives an automatic knows how to drive a car. I said, "You in touch with anybody from the old days?"

"Just what I read about Dee in the papers.

Denny lives in England, I think."

"I've had a hell of a time tracking people down."

"I'm not surprised," Cal said. "I mean, we all ran away after Lorraine died."

"Yeah, I guess."

"Jeff checked himself into McLean's. Guess he was afraid he might try to do himself in too."

"I can't remember Jeff's last name."

"Welch, I think. I wonder if he's still alive. Drove his car into a cement abutment, I heard. Maybe he liked hospitals."

I scooted around a slow VW, slid back into the right-hand lane.

"If Lorraine hadn't killed herself," Cal said with a sidelong glance at me, "we'd probably still be married. I'd have a steady job. Mild-mannered reporter, salesman, accountant. Maybe we'd have kids."

I got caught at a red light, a yellow, really. I would have blitzed through, but the guy in front of me stopped. "You laying all that at Lorraine's door?"

"Don't you? I remember that week like I remember yesterday. Maybe better. The funeral home. All those yellow chrysanthemums. I remember thinking, if life can end in one minute — so damn quickly with no damn warning — you better do what you want to do now, Calvin, right this minute. Because your next minute might not happen."

I was listening to Cal and keeping an eye out for potholes big enough to swallow my Toyota, but my mind kept swinging from Lorraine to Brenda, Brenda to Lorraine. One dead in a ratty apartment; one dead in a fancy hotel suite. Booze and pills. Pills and booze. And an injection.

"Dee ever use hard stuff when you were with her? Shoot up?"

Cal said, "I don't think so. Half the time I was so whacked out, I'm not sure what anybody else did. I'm not sure what I did."

I remembered Dee's odd small voice on the phone, sounding so far away, saying: "I should have called the doctor. Maybe she was alive."

Cal had me drive back and forth down Huntington, a challenge with all the potholes and trolley tracks. He did a lot of muttering, complained that he'd probably do better on foot. I drove the trolley route, stopping at all the train stops, asking questions. Do you remember this dry cleaner? This liquor store look familiar?

"Stop pushing," Cal said. "It'll come."

He told me to take a left near Parker Hill Hospital. We cruised the one-way streets until we passed a gravel parking lot, a rundown playground, a housing project.

"These trees," he said slowly. "I think I remember being with Davey, ducking behind these trees to take a leak."

"These particular trees?" I said skeptically. They didn't look remarkable to me.

"They smell bad. Ailanthus. City trees. You can't kill them. They grow through concrete. Turn left up here."

"Okay."

"One of these buildings," he said. "Something on this block anyway."

"Thanks," I said. "Truly." I maneuvered the car into a tight but legal slot. "Maybe this'll help."

"What are you going to do?" Cal said.

"Bump doors and ask if anybody remembers Davey."

"You gonna hire an armed guard?" he said, glancing around uneasily.

"I've worked tougher neighborhoods than this," I said, bristling.

"Yeah," he said, "but today you look like you spent the whole night doing what you were doing. You don't look like a cop."

"Cops don't screw?" I said.

"Don't yell at me. Can I come along? Maybe I'll recognize somebody. I think I'd remember this Malcolm guy."

I'm not sure he really wanted to do it. I don't think either of us had figured out a way to say good-bye. "I'll call you" didn't seem adequate or honest. "I won't call" seemed hard.

He took one side of the street and I took the other. My side had three-decker weathered gray buildings with maybe a two-foot span between them and the sidewalk, enough for a brownish patch of grass, an occasional half-dead bush. Cal's side was yellow brick apartments, bigger and built right up to the sidewalk.

People were hesitant to open their doors and I didn't blame them. I inquired for Dunrobie through half-inch slits. I asked for Malcolm. I asked if there was a vegetarian commune in the neighborhood.

I finished the block with no hint of success. Cal and I met at the corner.

"You find anything?" he asked.

"Nope," I said.

"I know we're close," he said.

"I've got other stuff to do," I said.

"How about if I keep looking?"

"I'm not asking you to."

"I know. But maybe it could count toward an apology."

"For?"

"It's one of the AA things. The twelve steps. Go back and apologize to the people you hurt when you were an addict."

"You can apologize if it makes you feel better," I said. "It doesn't change anything."

He walked away.

"Cal," I hollered after him. "I would appreciate it. I would deeply appreciate it if you'd help me find Davey."

CHAPTER TWENTY-SEVEN

Dee had moved down a floor to 718. She still rated a suite, but it wasn't half as grand as the last one. I used Mooney's name as a password to get by the two plainclothesmen guarding the door. I wondered if they were keeping Dee in or reporters out.

She wasn't alone.

Hal was hovering nervously over an elegant gent who sat bolt upright in an easy chair. I recognized him from the party: one of the men who looked like he'd stepped out of an ad for expensive evening wear. Maybe he was afraid his suit would wrinkle if he leaned back. Dee, forcing a smile, introduced him as Mr. Harvey Beringer, an executive vice-president of MGA/America, who just happened to be on his way out.

Mr. Beringer seemed surprised at the news of his departure. Dee looked like she was having a hard time controlling her temper.

"Great, Dee," Hal said sarcastically as Beringer banged the door shut.

"You're next," she said to Hal. "Scram."

Hal said, "I'm not going anywhere."

"Dee," I said, "I need a copy of that letter you showed me. From Lockwood."

"What? . . . Oh. I, uh, don't have a copy."

"Trust me with the original," I said. "I won't lose it."

"Hal, for chrissake," Dee said, "can't you just take a walk?"

"No way," he said. "You've got two more press guys and three more MGA reps to reassure. They're waiting."

"Dee," I said, "give me the letter."

"I told you to forget about it."

"Too late."

Her face didn't change, but her breath came a little faster. "Well, I don't know if I can find it, see?"

"Then just tell me the titles of the three songs," I said evenly.

She looked at me, a long, slow gaze, then she yanked open a dresser drawer, pawed under some scarves, and pulled out the envelope.

"I'm gonna pay him," she said. "Whatever he wants."

"Can you pound any sense through her thick skull?" Hal said to me, sinking down on the easy chair Mr. Beringer had vacated.

Dee paced the length of the room. Then she said, "Hal here thinks if I need money so badly, I should borrow it from a loan shark. You know, somebody who'll break my fingers if I come up short."

"Shut up," Hal said.

"You shut up," Dee replied bitterly. "First sign of trouble, and you're coming apart at the seams."

"First sign of — I like that! Never have I had somebody die on a tour of mine! Never!" There were two glasses on the marble-topped table next to the easy chair. Hal picked up one that was still full of amber liquid and downed it quickly.

"You know somebody in the loan business?" I asked Hal when he seemed to calm down a bit. "Somebody local?"

"A shark," Dee snapped.

"A friend," Hal said defensively. "A guy who's loaned me money in the past."

"Hal is a gamblin' man," Dee said, giving the words the same intonation she does on one of her songs. "He likes the part of the tour that goes through Atlantic City best."

"He knows about the money?" I asked.

"I know she's trying to make some dumb deal with MGA/America she's gonna regret for the rest of her life," Hal said. "You can get more than you're asking for, Dee. More money. More clout. You couldn't be hotter. If MGA doesn't want you, Capitol, RCA, anybody, will sign you. For a big fat advance."

Three hundred thousand seemed like a big, fat advance to me.

"Dee," I said, "in the letter, is he asking for the right amount?"

"What do you mean?"

I glanced over at Hal. He might know Dee needed money, but what else did he know? "Would a jury give him more?" I asked Dee. "Would a judge?"

"Hal," she said, "get the hell out of here. Now. Or I swear, you're fired."

He left, announcing that he'd be back in three minutes tops and slamming the door angrily.

"Three hundred thou is about right," Dee said, still holding on to the envelope, still pacing. "*If* he'd written the songs."

"Why? How would he come up with that number?"

"Mechanicals," she said.

I'd heard the term at the MGA party, but I still didn't understand it. "Explain," I said.

"You don't make money from royalties in the music business, not unless you're a superstar with a studio by the balls. You make money on what you write, especially songs other singers cover. Because for every copy of your song that's sold, you get your nickel. Or your two-point-five, depending."

"Depending?" I asked, more puzzled than before.

"Listen. You got your recording studio, your songwriter, your song publisher, and your singer. Let's forget about the singer for now. The songwriter's share is always a nickel. That's mechanical; it's carved in stone. If you keep your publishing rights, you get the whole nickel. Now, sometimes songwriters talk about 'losing' their publishing rights. If you lose your publishing rights, you get two-point-five cents a copy. The song publisher splits your nickel with you."

"How do you 'lose' your publishing rights?"

"A lot of companies put it right in the contract. They get the publishing rights, or you don't get to do the album. And you're young and stupid, and you don't know enough to hire a lawyer or a manager to tell you to hold out for the whole nickel. I lost the publishing on 'For Tonight.' If I lost the rest of the nickel on that one, I'd go broke. Thank God, you can't negotiate the two-point-five away. If you could, some maggot businessman would figure out how to nab it."

I shrugged my shoulders. "How does this add up to three hundred thousand?"

"Work it out. An album goes gold at five hundred thousand copies, platinum at a million. I write one song on a platinum album,

I earn twenty-five thousand dollars. You know how many golds and platinums 'For Tonight' wound up on?"

"Nope."

"Well, three hundred thousand dollars is just about what I've made on that song. It sounds like a lot, maybe, but it's come in dribs and drabs over, what? Twelve years. It's my living money."

"And the other two songs the lawyer mentioned?"

"Nobody else covers them. My money song's 'For Tonight.' "

"And Davey would be able to figure out how much you'd earned on it?"

"Anybody in the business could figure it out. But we're getting away from the point here. I wrote the goddamn song."

"But that's not the point, is it, Dee? That letter's not about mechanicals, or rights, or who wrote the songs."

"It says what it says," she answered after a long pause. She stopped pacing long enough to draw the drapes aside with her hand and stare down at the street below.

"Dee, don't do the MGA deal yet. Give me a little more time."

"To find Davey? Davey's gone nuts."

"Cal Therieux's out looking for him."

"Cal," she repeated slowly.

"Did you know he was here? How come you didn't tell me to start with him?"

She swallowed hard, let the drapes fall back in place. "We lost track," she said. "Just another boy who stole a little piece of my heart. How did Erma Franklin sing it? I always liked her version better than Janis Joplin's. 'Take it! Break another little piece — ' "

"Give me the letter, Dee."

"Why don't you just butt out of my life?"

"I can't believe how much I used to admire you."

"Yeah, well, that's because you didn't know me. You never saw anything but my hands on a guitar. You thought the songs I wrote were me. You still do, don't you?"

"Maybe."

"And maybe you still hate me a little for Cal, huh?"

"Maybe."

"So why the hell should I trust you?"

"Who else have you got?"

"Don't lose it," she said when she finally handed over the envelope.

As I left, I could hear her singing "Piece of My Heart." She was staring at herself in the full-length mirror on the back of the bathroom door.

Down in the lobby I used an elegant pay phone to ring Joanne at D Street.

"Mickey," I said. "Mickey who works for the Gianellis. He's a shark, right?"

"You broke down and asked the boy-friend?"

"I haven't even seen Sam," I said.

"Well, you're out of date. Mickey Manganero used to be a shark."

"Atlantic City?"

"Bingo. If that's the appropriate term."

"And now?"

"Skipped up the ladder. Money laundering. Nobody's sure how he handles it, but he seems to handle it in fairly big chunks."

"Drug money?"

"I can let you talk to a narc."

"No. Let it go for now. Mickey got a rap sheet?"

"Since Juvie Hall. That's sealed, but he's been busy ever since. Car theft, burglary, molestation. Almost got him on a rape. He likes young girls."

"How young?"

"Why don't you ask him? I'm sure the boy-friend can set up a meet."

"Maybe I will," I said.

CHAPTER TWENTY-EIGHT

I couldn't get an appointment with Stuart Lockwood. I couldn't get one under my own name. I couldn't get one by mentioning Dee Willis's name. I couldn't get one under an alias. Either business had improved dramatically or Lockwood was allergic to the sound of my voice.

I called Taylor Baines, of the gorgeous office and influential practice. The man who wanted to do his all for any artist employed by MGA/America.

Mr. Baines was cooperative. He had his efficient secretary telephone Stuart Lockwood's inefficient one. A suddenly liberated Lockwood assured Baines he could attend a three o'clock meeting with no difficulty.

Baines and I met in his lush office at two thirty. After politely offering coffee, which I accepted, he said to me, "I don't know about this. It's tough to throw a scare into a lawyer."

"There are lawyers, and then there are lawyers," I responded once the coffee lady had come and gone, silently leaving her tray of steaming china cups. "You already scared him. He's coming. And if he can be impressed, your office is the place to do it."

"It is rather nice, isn't it?" he agreed, taking time to stir his coffee and spin his leather chair to admire the view. The ocean was more blue than green today. The water closest to shore had a brownish cast. I wondered where they were digging the third harbor-tunnel.

"If I were trying to make it as a lawyer in this town, I'd want to do you a favor," I said.

"We do steer a lot of overflow business to smaller firms," he observed.

The secretary ushered Lockwood in at a quarter past three although I was sure he'd arrived earlier. Baines had given instructions not to bring him in until he'd cooled his heels in the outer office and had sufficient time to admire the floral arrangements, the original oil paintings, the rosewood furniture.

I'd briefed Baines, and he started off. I stayed in the room, but he didn't introduce me. Lockwood obviously thought I worked for the law firm, and his estimation of me skyrocketed. He smiled at me.

"I assume you're handling the Dunrobie case on a contingency basis," Baines began. He didn't offer Lockwood coffee even though our cups were still half full.

"I can't discuss that," Lockwood answered predictably.

"Then let's discuss blackmail," Baines said, with a perfectly charming smile.

"Blackmail," Lockwood repeated. He scratched his nose with his index finger, hurriedly stuck his hand in his lap when he realized what he'd done.

"The use of letters, containing threats and producing fear, to obtain money. Would you agree on the definition?" Baines said smoothly.

"Well, yes. On the definition."

"Blackmail is a criminal matter. When a blackmailing letter is sent through the mails, the charge of federal mail fraud can be appended." Baines took his time rereading the letter, then offered it to the lawyer. "I assume this is your letterhead and your signature."

Lockwood reread it carefully and nodded.

Baines said, "Then I can't really think of a good reason not to call the police. Maybe you can tell me one."

Lockwood wasn't worried yet. He said, "I believe it is customary, in any attempt to prove that a crime was committed, for the prosecution to show that there was both criminal intent and a wrongful overt act."

Baines held out his hand until Lockwood, somewhat reluctantly, handed back the sheet of stationery. "This paper would, I think, constitute a wrongful overt act. The only question is criminal intent."

"Whoa," Lockwood said, losing the casual air he was struggling to maintain, "you're talking crazy."

"Tell me about this client of yours and we'll see who's crazy," Baines said. "It won't look good when you're named as an accessory," he continued severely. "But perhaps this is your own idea, and there is no Mr. Dunrobie."

"What do you mean? Of course there's a Dunrobie."

"A man, I understand, with no telephone?"

"He calls me."

"And that doesn't seem odd to you?"

"I've only recently established my practice in this state. I can't pick and choose my clientele the way a more established lawyer might."

"And if you need to reach Mr. Dunrobie?"

"I can get in touch with him."

"At 825 Winter Street, Suite 505D?"

"How did you? — Did she? — That's a privileged communication — "

"Through what is known as a 'mail drop'?"

Lockwood hadn't known that; you could tell by his face. But he made a quick recovery. "He calls me, like I said."

"Have you ascertained — excuse me, did

you try to ascertain whether your client is a man of good faith? By that I mean, do you have the sense that he in fact knew Miss Willis?"

"Look, I don't take nuisance suits. I'm not an ambulance chaser."

"Then you did believe that this man was unlawfully done out of monies due him?"

"I did. I mean, the first time he showed up with his story, I gave him the brush-off. He looked too young, like he'd have been a kid when those songs were written. But then he came back with evidence that seemed to prove his case."

"What did he return with, exactly?"

Lockwood hesitated.

"Come, now. If you're going to be difficult, I'll simply file a discovery motion before we go to trial," Baines prompted.

"He showed me her photograph, suitably inscribed."

"I imagine she sends a great many photos to fans. What makes you think he's not some crank?"

"Look, if this is supposed to impress the hell out of me and make me tell him to drop the suit, forget it. The man has a valid case."

"So do we, against you, for federal mail fraud if nothing else."

I could see Lockwood's Adam's apple work. "Well," he said, "Mr. Dunrobie hasn't exactly given me the go-ahead to do this, but I'd rather settle out of court. He has given me a figure to shoot for. What he's got is the original sheet music to the songs. You know. His titles over her songs. The exact lyrics."

I said, "You can get note-for-note transcriptions through mail-order houses. And if the guy has musical training, if he has an ear, he could have transcribed her material himself and called it whatever he liked. It's not hard. All you have to do is buy a record."

"He also showed me self-addressed, postmarked, sealed envelopes — intact — that, he assures me, contain the identical songs."

"Have you had the postmarks authenticated?" I asked.

"A postmark is acceptable in a — "

"Sixteen-year-old kids know how to alter the birth dates on their driver's licenses," I interrupted. "It's even easier to change a postmark; mail's not laminated."

"I didn't see the need to involve experts until they were necessary," Lockwood said, not meeting my eyes. "My client didn't want expenses mounting up."

"Can you read sheet music?" I asked him.

"No."

"Have you had anyone who reads music take a look at this stuff?"

"Not yet."

"May I see it? Just the copies. I won't break into any sealed envelopes."

His eyes shifted to his briefcase. He'd brought the file along.

"We would appreciate it," Taylor Baines said into the growing silence.

Lockwood shuffled through his case, and finally handed over three Xeroxed pages, paper-clipped at the left-hand corner. I removed the clip, spread the sheets on the desk.

Baines raised his eyes questioningly to me.

"The Library of Congress accepts tapes for copyright purposes now, but they didn't ten years ago," I said. "Back then, a musician — even a musician who didn't read music — would get somebody to write out a lead sheet — that's the melody line. He might make it as simple as possible, or he might get fancy and stick in the tablature — that's a six-line staff that shows the guitar fingerboard." I tapped the pages on the desk in front of me. "But nobody who knew what he was doing would use this for copyright."

"Why?" Lockwood demanded. "What's wrong with it?"

"The sheet music for 'For Tonight' runs about six pages. I've seen it. I've played it. You've got three pages here."

"So, maybe it's a sample," he said.

"It's not the melody. It's not the lead sheet," I said. "All you've got here is the bass line."

"Are you sure?" Baines asked me.

I nodded, then said to Lockwood, "Did you know that Dee Willis's bass player is dead?"

Lockwood said, "I have no idea what you're talking about."

"Can you describe the man who came to you, who called himself David Dunrobie?"

"I only saw him twice."

"Short? Tall?"

"Short," Lockwood said, swallowing.

Baines and I exchanged glances.

"Did he limp?" I asked.

"No," Lockwood said. "He was short and I didn't notice anything odd about the way he walked."

"Then chances are," I said coldly, "he wasn't Davey Dunrobie."

CHAPTER TWENTY-NINE

"You can't squeeze blood from a turnip" was another of my grandmother's Yiddish standbys. It was fun to watch Taylor Baines try, but he couldn't get an address other than 825 Winter Street out of Stuart Lockwood, Esquire.

I went home. A man who was either a bold thief or a genuine locksmith was in the process of drilling out the main lock on my front door.

I introduced myself as the owner of the door.

"Closing up the barn after the horses, I understand," he said cheerfully. "Hi. Jack Daly. Gloria asked me to come by."

Roz appeared on the front stoop, looking particularly fetching in a fifties-vintage housedress, with a tomato-red apron around her waist, and sporting yellow rubber gloves. Electric eye-makeup, possibly left over from the night before, and her striped hair completed the look. "I did call somebody," she said defensively. "This guy just turned up first so I canceled the other one. Okay?"

"You have some ID?" I asked the lock-smith.

"Sure." He produced a printed business card, a driver's license.

"Pleased to meet you." We shook hands.

"Carlotta," Roz said, practically dancing in her impatience, "I gotta talk to you."

"I've been meaning to talk to you too."

She led me into the kitchen.

"I see my kitchen floor will never look the same," I said. All in all, that's not such a bad thing. It never looked great to begin with.

"Look," Roz said, "I know I screwed up about the locks, and about the red mailing tube, and about everything, but — "

"Hold that thought," I said. "I've got to make a phone call. I've got to call Gloria and — "

"Call Gloria! That's what I'm supposed to tell you!"

"So shut up a minute, and I will!"

When you call Green & White Cab, ninety percent of the time you get Gloria. She answers the phones, practically nonstop. I don't know when she has time to sleep, let alone attend to other body functions.

"Good to hear from you, babe," she said in as rich and fine a voice as you're likely to hear offstage.

"You send me a lock man? Jack Daly?"

"Yeah. My brother Leroy recommends him highly. Says he's good."

"White guy. Thirties? Sandy hair?"

"You gettin' cautious in your old age?"

"Hoping to stay alive long enough to enjoy one. Thanks."

"Don't hang up, babe. Sam asked me to call." Besides being my on-again, off-again boyfriend, Sam is also the co-owner of Gloria's cab company. He put up most of the money; she put up most of the savvy.

Sam's been scarce since he got back from Italy. I'm sure he met some hot madonna in Florence. My voice iced over. "He's got a tongue, and a phone as I recall," I said.

"Shut up and listen," Gloria said. "He wasn't sure his line was clear. He says he heard your name come up in a bad situation."

"Great. What kind of a message is that?"

"He's gonna try to take care of it, but he says you might want to back off."

" 'Back off.' Very nice. I appreciate that. 'Back off' is what some goon wrote on my bathroom mirror last night. If Sam Gianelli knew about it — "

"Whoa, babe. When he came by this morning, I told him about somebody trashing your place. He made a few calls. That's where he got this. He didn't know anything last night. You two still seeing each other or what?"

Gloria likes to keep tabs on my love life.

"You wouldn't believe me if I told you," I said. She never liked Cal.

"Go on, tell me anyway," Gloria said. "You want to come by, do some driving tonight?"

"Can't."

"You sound troubled, babe."

"I am, and not about my love life either."

"What else is there?" Gloria asked. She reads romance magazines when she's not answering the phone.

"Lots." Like pairing up Hal Grady with Mickey Manganero. Quite a team. One man who moves money for the mob, another who handles receipts for a hot ticket like Dee.

"Look," I said to Gloria. "Let me try out a couple questions. Who handles your night deposits?"

"I suppose you got a good reason for asking."

"Trust me," I said.

"My brother Leroy comes by. I figure nobody's gonna mess with Leroy."

"Are you or Sam or Leroy on some kind of exempt list, for making large deposits without filing one of those government forms?"

"The bank only has to fill in the blanks whenever somebody deposits or withdraws ten thou or more. We don't turn that kind of cash at night with only eight vehicles on

the road. I'm not on any exempt list and neither is Sam, far as I know."

"Who would be on the exempt list?"

"Grocery stores. Sports stadiums, for sure.
Fenway takes in more than ten thousand every
time the Red Sox lose one."

"What bank do you do business with?"

"Bank of New England."

"Got a friend there?"

There is no place Gloria doesn't have a
friend. She gave an affirmative grunt over the
line.

"See if you can find out where the Berklee
Performance Center makes deposits, okay?
And the name of the guy on the exempt list
would be a real bonus."

"I'll see what I can come up with. Take
care, now."

Roz said, "Seriously, I think I found something important."

"It's hard to take somebody seriously," I
said to Roz, "when they dress like Donna
Reed on speed."

"Well, can I at least show you what I
found?"

"Looks like you discovered a brand-new
layer of kitchen floor. You taking up arche-
ology?"

Roz said, "What do you think of this?"

"I think it's a dustpan," I said. "I'm glad

you found it. Do you know how to use it?"

"Shit. Look inside, Carlotta. I'm not fooling around here."

She carefully positioned the dustpan on the kitchen counter, a place where I frequently eat my meals, not always taking time for a sit-down dinner. I wondered if Roz would wash the counter off afterward. I wondered if I'd ever be able to eat there again without thinking of the filthy gray dustpan.

In the tray were three blonde hairs.

"You haven't swept the floor since you were a blonde?" I guessed. "How long ago is that? Two months?"

"These were stuck in the goo in the kitchen. If you'll take a good look, you'll see they're longer than my hair's ever been."

I picked one out of the tray. "Curly," I said.

"Dyed," Roz said. "Permed. Heat-damaged, like from a crimping iron. You know somebody with hair like that?"

I trust Roz on matters of hair. Anyone who spends the kind of time on dye jobs that she does ought to know her stuff. "You know, Roz, you have just taken a long step on the road to redemption."

She beamed. Roz likes living where she does, likes her work, or lack of it.

"Of course," I said, half to myself, "the next step is a lulu."

That's when the doorbell interrupted. I figured it was the locksmith. I was wrong. The locksmith could have let himself in.

CHAPTER THIRTY

"Come with me," I said to Roz on my way to answer the bell. We hadn't finished our chat, and it never hurts to have a karate expert tag along.

Cal was idling on the stoop, trading August heat tales with the locksmith.

I flashed on the chorus of Dee's song "For Tonight."

"For tonight, for a while, I want you."

Last night I had practically ached to touch him, from the moment he'd walked onstage, eyes downcast, from the moment he'd thumbed his first note.

But not tonight. Definitely not for a string of nights.

"I found him," Cal said.

It wasn't what I'd expected him to say. His voice sounded funny.

"Davey?"

"Davey."

"Terrific. Wonderful. Where? Come on in and tell me the whole story. I'll get you a drink, uh, a soft drink. Orange juice."

"No. I, uh, I'd rather not."

"Well, where is he?"

"We have to go there."

"Cal? Are you okay?"

"We have to go there," he repeated, his tone harsh, almost angry. He stared at the steps. I couldn't see his eyes.

"Now?"

"Yeah. Now would be good."

One look at the set of Cal's jaw, and I knew I'd get no further with questions. "Okay, be like that," I said. "Roz, have you ever considered a future as a groupie?"

"That's not a future, that's a past."

"Dress weird," I said. "Hell, dress normally. And get over to the Four Winds Hotel. Seventh floor, some of them may still be on the eighth, but the seventh's your best bet. Tell anybody who asks that you're with Dee Willis's band. The drummer's name is Freddie. Ron's the lead guitar. I don't know the keyboard man. He seems to evaporate into thin air every time I come near. Hal Grady's the road manager."

"Yeah. Ron and Freddie and Hal. Which one am I interested in?"

"None of the above. Get tight with a camp follower named Mimi. Looks sixteen. Dyed blonde curly hair."

"Oooh," said Roz, "long hair. I get it. I'm

your undercover agent."

I blew out a deep breath. "Keep it that way, Roz," I said. "I want to know everything about this girl — who she talks to, who she sleeps with, whether she deals, what she deals, whether she uses, what she uses. I want you to be her new best friend."

"And if some of the boys come on to me?"

"That's your business. Just make sure you're with Mimi most of the time."

"I'll be great," Roz promised. "I know the exact outfit. I'll make up for the tube and the locks — "

"Whoa, Roz. Don't go in like a sledgehammer, okay? Be subtle. It could be dangerous."

"If she's the one messed up the kitchen floor," Roz said, peeling off her rubber gloves, "it could be fucking dangerous for her."

CHAPTER
THIRTY-ONE

"Why are you looking for Davey?" Cal slammed the passenger door of my red Toyota and made a grab for the seat belt. He used to swear I was the reason he never learned to drive.

"What difference does it make? You didn't ask last night — or this morning."

"I'm asking now."

"I was hired to find him."

"By?"

"A client."

I remembered last night's taxi ride in the pouring rain, my intense awareness of Cal's wet denim jacket, the bass jutting between his legs, his thigh pressed close to mine, the strangely familiar smell of him. In daylight, in the front seat of my own car, everything seemed different, all tension spent. Maybe that was all we ever shared, the tension and release, tension and release of coupling. Possibly the tension would build again over the next few hours.

I doubted it.

"Is Davey in jail?" I asked.

"No."

"Is he alive?"

"You could say so."

"Come on, Cal. No more guessing games."

"I think I'm the one who's doing most of the guessing here, Carly."

"I can't help what you think, Cal."

I turned the key in the ignition, counted to an imaginary ten, and held my temper. "It would help if I knew where we were going."

"Saint John of God Hospital."

"On Allston Street?"

"Yeah."

"But that's a — "

"A hospice." Cal finished the sentence before I could get the word out. Staring through the windshield, his face a mask, he said, "Davey's dying. Davey's got AIDS."

CHAPTER THIRTY-TWO

I have trouble with hospitals. Big deal, right? Who doesn't? I especially have trouble with the idea of a hospice — a hospital of no return. Even when I knew beyond doubt, beyond reason — confirmed by every doctor worth his stethoscope — that this attack of emphysema was Dad's final round, there was still that tiny undeniable ray of hope. Maybe this time, this once, one puny human will confound the experts and defy the odds.

My dad's Scots-Irish Catholic family believed in miracles; maybe they passed that on to me. My mom believed God had cleared out of the miracle business, left people to create their own if they could. She also believed human beings had gravely disappointed their maker.

The only miracle I was praying for was that Cal's informant had made a mistake.

St. John of God Hospital is a small place that keeps a low profile. Unless you drive directly down Allston Street between Summit Avenue and Washington Street, you'd never know it existed. It's on a taxi route, a good shortcut between Brookline and Cambridge; otherwise I'd never have heard of it, much less known the way there.

I pulled my Toyota into the cement square of parking lot. There weren't many cars.

The lobby looked too cheery, like Christmas in August. The front desk was staffed by two women, one heavy, one thin. The thin one wore a cardigan sweater in spite of the heat, and was busily filing a broken fingernail; the plump one was tapping at a computer keyboard.

I caught a faint quiver of interest when I asked for David Dunrobie.

"He doesn't get many visitors," I ventured.

"You're the only ones I've seen," the woman working at the terminal replied. The other woman nodded her head in solemn agreement.

"Are there, like, visiting hours?" Cal said. He'd stayed half a foot behind me. I could hear the faint snap of his fingers, a nervous habit I'd long forgotten.

The thin woman picked up a phone receiver and said, "Let me check whether one of Mr. Dunrobie's doctors is available. See if it's a good day for a visit."

"Sometimes he's not well enough for visitors?" Cal asked, a little too quickly.

The heavy woman at the keyboard exchanged a glance with the nail-filer, then spoke in a confidential whisper. "He's got a sort of, uh, amnesia, as a symptom of the disease. He fades in and out. Some days he talks up a storm. Some days . . ." She shrugged her massive shoulders.

Suddenly I didn't want to see him. I wanted to keep a picture of him in my mind: Davey Dunrobie, young, talented, graceful, on his way to the top.

Cal voiced my misgivings. "Do we need to do this?"

"I have to," I said. "You can wait for me, take a walk, go home, whatever."

The thin woman murmured, "Here comes the doctor now." I noticed that her nail file had disappeared discreetly into a pocket. She bent her head and diligently sorted forms.

The man in the white lab coat, white shirt, and red bow tie had entered the lobby through swinging doors. The nameplate on his breast pocket read: Dr. Sanderley. He spoke in a reedy tenor. "Are you related to Mr. Dunrobie?" he asked.

"Close friends," I said. "We just found out."

"He's been with us six months," the doctor replied.

"Off and on?" I asked.

"Six months."

"Does he go out much? Travel?"

"I'm not sure I understand," the doctor said. "When he goes out, which isn't frequently, it's in a wheelchair. Sometimes we get a chair-van for day trips. Not often." He seemed puzzled by my questions.

"How is he?" I said. The doctor seemed more comfortable with that one.

He consulted his wristwatch as if to figure out exactly how much detail he could fit into his schedule. "Well, he's had several bouts of pneumonia," he began. "Pneumocystic, the kind most HIV patients get. Each attack has left him a bit weaker, more open to other infections. He had a go with meningitis. He has thrush, an infection that interferes with the clarity of his speech."

"Break it to us gently, doc," Cal muttered in a bitter tone I remembered like a whiplash.

"I'm sorry," the doctor said gently, taking no offense. "But if you intend to see him, you ought to be prepared. He's also losing his eyesight. And in addition to attacking the immune system, HIV may also attack and destroy brain cells, causing dementia."

"The nurse up front told us he sometimes had amnesia," I said.

"She's not a nurse; she's a receptionist. And she has no business discussing the patients. Absolutely no business." Doctor Sanderley's anger subsided abruptly. "It's often difficult to get good people to work in a place like this," he said with a sigh.

I swallowed. "Does Davey know where he is? What's happening to him?"

"Sometimes, yes. Sometimes, no."

I bit my lip. "Look, I need to see him."

"You *need* to see him? This isn't a social call?"

"It may be a police matter," I said. If I'd had the photostat of my license, the one in my stolen purse, I'd have shown it to him. All I had was a business card. "I'd like to keep the police out of it."

"Would Mr. Dunrobie recognize your names?"

"If he recognizes anything. Tell him Carlotta and Cal are here."

"I'll try."

We were left in the lobby for five minutes, maybe four, maybe fewer, but it felt like forever. I had time to memorize the burgundy carpet, the blue sofas and chairs, the framed landscapes, the portraits of long-dead benefactors. There were too many vases of overblown flowers in the room, too many smelly plants.

The double doors opened and the stink of disinfectant invaded my nostrils. I thought of Dee in her four-star hotel suite, Davey in his hospice bed. A lucky toss of the dice. An unlucky one.

Dr. Sanderley led us through the double doors and down a long corridor. Women in white slacks and bright-colored T-shirts hurried by in rubber-soled shoes.

Sanderley hesitated before a door labeled 101A. "Go ahead in. I'm not sure how much he'll say or how responsive it might be, but there's no reason not to visit." He smiled encouragingly. "I'll come by in a while if I can get away."

I braced myself, the way I used to when I wore the uniform, when I had to stand watch over a stiff until the homicide detectives came to take charge — before I became a homicide detective myself.

Then I was inside, staring at the name on the chart at the foot of the bed, straining to believe, trying to disbelieve, that this was the man, the boy, I'd known. His head was a skull. He was so thin his forearms looked breakable, like matchsticks. His eyes burned. Then, suddenly, he smiled at me, at Cal, and his bloodless lips had to stretch to cover the width of the grin.

"Long time," Davey said. "Oh, boy, long time. Carlotta, Dee, Cal, Lorraine, the old gang."

I had to lean forward to hear his cracked voice.

"Yeah," Cal said. He walked right over and shook Davey's outstretched hand. I did the same. It felt like a bird's wing. I barely touched it.

Tubes dripped clear liquids into the veins of his left arm; urine dripped into a plastic bag attached to the mattress of the mechanical bed.

"Davey," I said, "I didn't know. I didn't know anything about what happened to you after the group disbanded, after Lorraine died, until this week, until Dee told me."

"Dee's swell. Man, anytime I need anything, you know, I got a famous friend. Did I tell you I know Dee Willis? Man, I'm practically responsible for Dee Willis."

"Here we go again." I hadn't even realized Davey wasn't in a private room until I heard the other voice. His roommate was a tiny wizened man. I was afraid even to guess his age because he looked well over sixty and I was pretty certain he wasn't yet forty.

I rounded on him. "What do you mean?"

"Hi," he said. "My name's Mike. I used to be with the Merchant Marine. That's why I've got the travel posters all over the walls. Every place you see, I've been, some twice."

"They're great posters, Mike," I said. "What did you mean by that 'Here we go again'?"

"It's not so bad really. I've had worse roomies than Davey here. It's just every once in a while he gets on this Dee Willis rag, and you can't stop him. He talks about her for hours on end. Same stuff over and over. I mean, I talk about some of the best ports I ever landed in, but at least I only tell the same story once."

In his whispery voice, Davey said, "I knew Dee when she was nobody. Nobody. She made me fuckin' famous, 'cause I'm the first guy she ever slept with, you know that?"

In a bored voice, Mike said, "Yeah, Davey, I know you slept with Dee Willis. You sleep with Dolly Parton? Cher? Were they the greatest or what? You can tell me all about them too."

"Davey was Dee Willis's singing partner," I said with enough volume for Mike to hear. "She hired me to find him. Davey, do you understand? Dee told me to find you."

I looked up at Cal. He'd frozen at the mention of Dee's name.

Davey started to cry, but it wasn't really crying. It was more an overflow of tears, as if he couldn't control his eyes anymore.

Doctor Sanderley said softly, "That happens a lot. Emotional control goes. Don't let it bother you. It doesn't bother him."

I hadn't even heard the doctor enter the room.

Davey said, "Sweet Lorraine. I gotta stop talking about Lorraine and Dee. I know that, man. But Dee, shit, maybe Dee shouldn't have laid that on me. I mean, I hear Dee on the radio, man, I see her on TV. I hear Dee all the time, singing to me, singing those songs for me."

I didn't think it would do any good, but I decided to ask. "Davey, did you write any of Dee's songs?"

He looked at me and said clearly, "Maybe one chord. Maybe nothing. Dee sang to me. Dee sang to me like a bird in a tree once. I love Dee like my mother, like my sister, like my baby, my lover. Dee sings me songs on the radio."

Mike, the roommate, laughed. "Yesterday he told me he wrote everything she ever sang. He said if he had his rights he'd have maybe three, four hundred thousand bucks."

"Really?" I said. "He mentioned that figure?"

"Just about all the time. Three hundred thousand smackers. Do a lot of first-class travel on that kind of bread."

I turned back to Davey. "Does Dee give you money?"

"If I ever need money, Dee gives me money. Man, all I ever have to do is ask. Dee, she'd give me anything."

"Have you talked to her lately?"

"No."

"Why would Dee give you anything, Davey?"

"Shhh," he said. "Secret, secret."

"Come on, Davey," I said. "It's me, Carlotta. It's Cal. We won't tell."

"You'll tell," he said in his eerie ruined voice. I wondered if it hurt him to speak. "Dee, she'll get angry. Throw one of those fits. You know how she is."

"No, Davey, she told me to find you. Dee wants me to know."

"I'm not telling," he said, narrowing his eyes cannily. "I know what you're doing. You're not even here, right? It's those drugs, right? They make me talk all the time, say all this stuff. I never knew her, really. Just knew sweet Lorraine, that's all, just sweet Lorraine."

The roomie said, "It goes on like this for hours. Sometimes he sings. That's a real treat."

"Does he have a guitar?" I asked.

The doctor shook his head.

"He used to play. If he had one, do you think he might like to, I don't know, just hold it, or play it or something?"

"He might," the doctor said.

"Could he, with all that junk in his arm?"

"I'm not sure," the doctor said.

"I'll bring his over," Cal said.

"No, Cal," I said. "Let me bring him mine."

"I'll bring his Hummingbird, Carly. Shut up."

Davey said, "Did I ever tell you about the night Dee and I got so drunk we couldn't stand up onstage? We had to play our guitars standing back-to-back so we could hold each other up."

The roomie said, "Yeah, Davey, you told me that. Doc, you think I can get another roommate? Somebody who's done a little traveling? Somebody knows where Singapore is?"

Davey rambled on about Malcolm, his guru on the hill, and other people we didn't know. He started to cry again when he said he couldn't find his old pictures, his photos of Dee and the gang. He accused Mike of stealing them, and Mike put his pillow over his ears and repeated his request for a new roommate.

"I'd like a little intelligent conversation before I die," Mike said. His last word seemed to echo off the walls.

When Cal and I left we weren't sure Davey knew we'd gone. We weren't sure he knew we'd been there.

"Is there anything I can do?" I asked Sanderley out in the hall. "Does he have a radio, a tape deck?"

"We have good sound equipment. Donated."

I'd get him a tape of Dee's latest album. Maybe Dee could send a tape of the concert.

"Anything else?"

"He likes mocha almond ice cream," Dr. Sanderley said.

"Mocha almond," I echoed.

"To tell the truth," Sanderley said, softening his words with his gentle smile, "there's not a lot anybody can do for him. Just accept him the way he is." The doctor's nostrils flared in a well-disguised yawn, and I wondered how long it had been since the man had slept.

CHAPTER THIRTY-THREE

Cal and I beat a shaky retreat through the lobby. I knew I'd have to go back and ask more questions, but I needed fresh air. Neither of the receptionists glanced up. Maybe they were used to friends and family leaving in a blind rush.

"Cal?"

He walked to a bench between two tall yews and sat as if his legs had decided they couldn't bear his weight. He dug his heels into the turf and stared at a spot between his feet.

I stared at the grass for a while too. Then at the cloudy sky. I remembered the crummy apartment Dee and Davey shared on Mass. Ave. Their only real piece of furniture, a saggy davenport, had been covered with a fringed brown slipcover. They used a tiny electric space-heater for a fireplace.

Cal said belligerently, "I found him for you, what's left of him. Isn't it time you told me what the hell's going on?"

"I'm just starting to figure it out myself," I said carefully. "I thought when I found

265

Davey, I'd find all the answers."

"Have you?"

"Maybe."

"Maybe," he repeated.

"Maybe," I echoed.

When Cal started to speak again it was in a voice almost as soft as Davey's, like he'd forgotten about me and was thinking out loud. "I could be in that room. When I was tanked, I did speedballs, junk, anything I could get my hands on. I shot up with people I wouldn't want to stand next to on the subway."

"Yeah," I said, to remind him I was there.

He shook his head, rubbed his hands across his eyes like he wanted to blot out what he'd just seen. "I hope you're not worried about last night, Carly. I have been tested."

"Cal, I'm not worrying about last night. I'm worrying about fifty-seven other things. I'm worrying about Davey. I'm wondering if Sanderley knows what he's talking about when he says there's nothing anybody can do."

"You talking last-ditch experimental drugs? Think Davey would want that? The way he is? Sometimes here, sometimes there?"

"Wouldn't we have to ask him when he's here?"

"Shit, Carly, this place gives me the creeps. Let's go, okay? I'll get Davey's guitar."

I dug the keys to my Toyota out of my

pocket. "You really have a driver's license?"

"What?"

"Take my car, pick up the guitar, and come back. If I'm not here, leave the car in the lot."

"Keys?"

"Put the keys in the glove compartment and lock it. I've got another set. Don't get side-swiped and don't leave the car unlocked for a second."

"Come with me," Cal said.

"I can't."

"Why?"

"Because people who work in hospitals know where to get syringes."

CHAPTER THIRTY-FOUR

One of the receptionists coughed when I pushed the double doors open, but she didn't say anything or do anything to stop me. I never saw Dr. Sanderley. I strolled the halls, looking for a familiar face, a face I might have seen at Dee's hotel or at the Berklee Performance Center rehearsal. I didn't see one.

I climbed a staircase, found a pleasant enough solarium on the second floor. A few of the stronger-looking patients — some with crutches, some in wheelchairs — were hanging out, laughing at a TV talk show. Two men in bathrobes were playing gin rummy across a card table.

I kibitzed a hand or two. My mother taught me two card games, pinochle and rummy. My father said she cheated at both.

"You a do-good lady?" one of the cardplayers asked. He had splotches the size of nickels on both his hands and wrists, up to where they disappeared into the bathrobe sleeves. The other player regarded me quizzically.

"Nope," I said. "Definitely not a do-good lady."

"They come around," one of the TV-watchers said.

"You a relative?" another TV-viewer asked.

"Friend. Davey Dunrobie. Old friend."

"Lucky him," muttered a man as bald as an egg.

I said, "A young girl work here, come by to visit? I don't know, she could be a nurse's aide or a volunteer. Sixteen, seventeen years old. Pretty sensational-looking. Curly blonde hair?"

The men exchanged glances.

One guy replied in an exaggeratedly fey voice. "I only notice the boys, sweetheart," he said. Another man laughed. I got the feeling it was an ongoing joke.

A cardplayer said, "None of the do-good ladies looks like that. And none of the nurse's aides. Trust me, I'd notice."

I tried another tack. "Davey told me there was this one, I don't know, maybe nurse or orderly, he really liked." I did my best to give a verbal picture of the guy I'd last heard described as Brenda's "boy-toy." Slender, young, maybe foreign. I remembered his dark, smudgy eyes.

"Ray?" the other cardplayer said sharply.

"That jerk? He was actually nice to somebody?"

"Ray," I said. "Yeah, that's the guy. Where could I find him?"

"He quit," one of the TV-watchers said. "He was an orderly. He gets to quit. Walk out the door."

"You know Ray's last name?" I ventured.

"Nope. And I don't care either."

The heavyset receptionist, the one who talked too much, was handling the front desk alone. She hadn't gotten her lecture on confidentiality from Doctor Sanderley yet. I gave her a song and dance about how Davey had asked me to send Ray a remembrance when he died. She gave me Ray's last name along with his home address.

CHAPTER
THIRTY-FIVE

I dialed the station from a public phone in the lobby, hoping Cal and my car would re-appear while the police kept me on hold. No one could find Mooney. He was away from his desk, which could mean anything from a quick trip to the men's room to chasing down a hot lead on Brenda's death. Maybe he'd fi-nally gone home to face his dragonlady mother and get some sleep. Joanne was not available. I hesitated over leaving Ray Daggett's name and address with the desk sergeant. With some trepidation, I phoned Mooney's apartment, and naturally got the dragonlady, who in-formed me she wouldn't dream of waking her boy for a call from the likes of me.

She disapproved of me when I was a cop because, she told me, women aren't meant to be policemen. She still dislikes me now that I'm no longer a cop. I'm beginning to take it personally.

I left Ray's name and address with Mom. She might hate me, but she'd make sure Moo-ney got it. I clinched that by telling her it might help his chances for promotion. She fancies herself as the mother of the police commissioner. Mooney just laughs it off.

My Toyota didn't show, so I dialed Gloria at Green & White Cab, searching my pockets for dimes, nickels, and quarters to feed the phone.

"I need a ride at Saint John's on Allston Street," I said when she picked up on the second ring.

"The hospital? You okay?"

"Fine. Any news for me?"

"I found out a couple things," Gloria said casually, as if she really weren't proud of being one of the best-connected gossips in town, which she is. "Berklee Performance Center keeps their cash right next door at Bank of Commerce. Man listed on the exempt sheet is one of their regular security people, George Wolfe, with an *e* on the end."

"Thank you." I remembered Dee's unflattering description of security at the Performance Center.

"Wait up, babe. Best is yet to come. Paolina called me."

It made my mouth dry. I swallowed. "Paolina?"

"That's what I said. Her mom won't let her call *you*, but she knows her way around a phone book, and she figured that 'no calls' didn't extend to roundabout messages. She says thank you kindly for the kite. Says she got it up about a mile in the sky this morning. Says she hoped you saw it."

I found myself smiling for the first time since I'd heard about Davey. "If she calls again, tell her I'll look for it. Tell her . . . Thanks, Gloria."

"Yeah," she said, her voice a little gruffer than usual. "You need anything else, you let me know."

"Just send the cab, okay?"

Getting by the cops on the hotel room door wasn't hard this time. I knew one of them. My acquaintance nodded at me and said, "This one's okay," to her beefy partner. He barely grunted, but he gave me the once-over and I was sure he'd recognize me the next time we met.

Dee was picking at the Reverend's old Gibson, humming a tune under her breath. I realized I hadn't seen her alone for more than a few minutes since the night she'd ventured so disastrously into the park, the night she'd hired me. My eyes did a quick search, but the room seemed empty. A pack of Marlboros, my dad's poison of choice, sat on a low table near Dee's chair. The ashtray had long since overflowed.

Dee remembered her burning cigarette,

took a puff, stuck the butt under a string near a tuning peg. She fingered a B flat the hard way, looked over her shoulder, and attempted a smile when she saw me.

"Jimmy says keep on playing, get on with the tour, don't miss a date, or I'll never get the chance again," she muttered over a progression of chord changes.

"Got a bass player?"

"Jimmy's flying in two from the coast. Both veteran session men. One's from a glitter-rock band, but Jimmy swears he's okay on the blues." She tried her smile out again. "I say only the broads in my band get to use makeup. He wears the teensiest bit of eye shadow, we go with the other one, even if he can only play in A."

I made sure the door was closed, bolted it from the inside. "Dee," I said, "this tour may stop before it starts."

She ignored me. I'm not even sure she heard me. "You know that song?" she asked. "Old song. 'Wild Women Don't Get the Blues'?"

"Dee?"

"Well, it's crap, Carlotta. A load of crap."

"I found Davey," I said. "Have you been drinking?"

" 'Oh, baby, I been drinkin' ' " She sang Randy Newman's line, trying to look unconcerned. "I told you, forget about him."

I sat down on the couch, uninvited. "MGA/America's attorney didn't agree with you."

She shrugged as if nothing mattered anymore, sat tall in her straight-backed chair, and fingered a familiar riff, the opening to Danny O'Keefe's "Steel Guitar." She started singing before I could interrupt.

"Carol once told me she dreamed
she was pretty,
Lived in a very cool part of the city,
With a man who came home every
evening at six,
And begged her to play him
his favorite licks,
On a steel guitar, on a real guitar,
She could put it all together on a real,
on a steel guitar."

"Remember that one?" she said, keeping the rhythm going. "Dum, dum, dum da da dum. I've been thinking of opening with it."

I unfolded the letter from Stuart Lockwood, held it so she couldn't avoid seeing it. "Lorraine ever sing it with you?" I asked. " 'Sweet Lorraine,' 'Missing Note,' 'Duet.' It was all in the song titles in the lawyer's letter, right? There was never any plagiarism."

275

"Plagiarism is what the letter said," she responded slowly, staring down at Miss Gibson, her fingers moving along the strings like they were separate creatures with minds of their own. "Sing it with me, Carlotta. Try Lorraine's part."

> " 'Cause her daddy'd been a welder
>   during the war,
> And he played country music every
>   night till four,
> With some drugstore cowboys who could
>   pick and grin,
> And if you let it all out, they'd bring it
>   all back in.
> On a steel guitar, on a real guitar,
> 'Cause they could put it all together
>   on a steel,
>   on a real guitar."

"Dee," I said. "Stop it. What happened to Lorraine? *Sweet Lorraine?*"
She just sang louder, and I gave up and joined in, faintly at first.

> "He taught his daughter to drink whiskey
>   like water,
> To go for the man with something
>   to offer,
> He said to her, baby, you can

go very far,
With an easy laugh and a steel guitar.
That steel guitar, that real guitar,
You don't need a man, you got a real,
you got a steel guitar."

"Did you kill Lorraine?"

Dee hugged the guitar like a shield, cutting off the song mid-note. "Oh, sweet Jesus, Carlotta, no."

"Just no. That's it?"

"It was suicide. Cross my heart. Suicide."

I waited. Silence was usually the best technique with a suspect, but Dee had the perfect defense, the guitar. "Dammit, you made me forget," she said. "What's the next verse, Carlotta? Please."

I didn't answer.

"Please."

"Jack," I said, reluctantly.

"Yeah," she said. "Old Jack."

"Jack was a rambler,
he'd been around Nashville,
He knew all the tricks
and he sure wasn't bashful.
He heard Carol playing steel guitar.
He said to her, baby,
you and me could go far.
On a steel guitar, on a real guitar,

Let's put it all together on a real,
on a steel guitar."

"Dee," I said insistently.
"One more verse. The killer verse."

"I'll make a long story short,
they had a couple of children,
Jack went to war and the enemy killed him.
Carol got his pension and his Purple Heart,
And now every evening till two she just
picks him apart.
On a steel guitar, on a real guitar,
She says I don't need a man,
I got a real, I got a steel guitar."

She finished with a flourish, whining the
last note up the neck of the old guitar. "Think
I can open with that?" she said. "Funny and
sad? Or you think it's too bitter?"

"Talk to me, Dee. About sweet Lorraine."

When she started to play again, I clamped
my right hand over the strings.

"Shit," she said.

"Talk," I said.

She laid the guitar in her lap, ran her fingers
soundlessly over the frets. "I was there," she
said finally, her voice as empty as her face.
"That's all. I was there. I slept at Lorraine's
that night. We drank wine, and I felt woozy,

and I passed out. I think she put stuff — pills, something — in our drinks. When I woke up, she was dead. I got out of there."

"Why?"

"Why? Because I was young, and I was scared. I ran to Davey. Davey was living at my place, remember? I was supposed to spend the night with him. He was waiting when I got home."

"Was Lorraine dead when you left?"

"Don't you think I've asked myself that a thousand times? Was she dead? I thought so. I'm ninety-nine percent sure she was dead. The whole thing, it happened so long ago. . . . It didn't seem real. It still doesn't. Sometimes I'm playing a bar — or driving — and I swear I see her . . . But it's never her."

She swallowed. "Davey knew I ran away. And he knew about the suicide note."

" 'Missing note,' " I said. Another phony song title.

Dee tried the bridge to "Steel Guitar" again, staring at her hands so she wouldn't have to look at me. "Yeah. Lorraine left a note, a last letter to me. A letter about me."

I saw the photo of Lorraine at the picnic in my mind. So young.

"See, we had this thing, Lorraine and me, while I was with Davey. You gotta remember, I was still a kid from backwoods Missouri.

I didn't know about gays, lesbians, whatever. I was just pretty damned naïve. I was fooling around with sex was all. I did that a lot, fooled around, with all kinds of sex. And Lorraine, she's like in love with me. That's what she kept saying that last night, she's in love with me, and she's gonna be mine forever. We'll be together forever eternally."

Dee half sang the last sentence like a mocking children's song. When she started to talk again, her voice was cool, distant, and angry.

"Well, I told her it wasn't that way with me. I told her it wouldn't even make a halfway decent lyric. Too crappy sentimental. Together, forever, June, moon, spoon. I don't do that kind of shit. I wasn't gonna be true to her; I wasn't gonna be true to Davey. Hell, I'm not proud of it. I'm just not that kind of person. I wasn't made that way. I wasn't nasty to Lorraine. I told her I liked her fine. I said we could fool around when I was in town, but I had plans for the road, and I liked men too. Liked men better."

"What did Lorraine say?"

"That she knew I'd come around; that we were perfect singing partners."

"Duet." The third bogus song title.

"She said we'd do music together," Dee went on, "*her* kind of music. She thought maybe we'd join one of those women's music labels, like Yolanda, or Lady Godiva, or whatever. One of those goody-good labels where the artists back causes and never earn a dime. Do music about 'our love.' "

"Uh-huh," I said quietly, to keep her talking.

"I told her it wasn't gonna happen. She killed herself. She left a note."

"And Davey knew about the suicide note?" While I asked, I realized I wasn't absorbing answers. I was just hearing about suspects and perps like when I was a cop. I wasn't thinking about my Lorraine, the first death I'd mourned, or my Davey, the Davey I'd slept with, or my Dee, the best singer I'd ever backed on rhythm guitar.

She responded bitterly, "Sure Davey knew, with me just about passed out on the floor. I couldn't even get the words out, couldn't make myself say it: Lorraine is dead. The letter was in my hand. I held it out to him. He read it. He kept it."

"Why didn't you tell me, Dee?" I kept my voice low, but I couldn't keep the anger out of it. "Why didn't you tell me?" All those years wondering why Lorraine killed herself. All those years of guilt. And I never would have guessed the truth. I saw Lorraine's plain oval face, her smooth brown hair. Heard her clear soprano voice. I'd known her for what?

two, three years. And never suspected she was gay. Certainly never suspected she loved Dee Willis.

"Oh, sure," Dee said, "tell little Miss Cop. You would have gotten me busted for sure. Made me turn that awful letter over to the police, the whole thing. You know what a rumor like that could do back then? Dee Willis, the singer, she sleeps with chicks? Chick even killed herself over Dee Willis. Believe me, I never wanted to come out of any closet, Carlotta. I had a tour planned. I had management. I thought I was going someplace big in a hurry."

She reached into the guitar case and picked up her bottleneck slide. "It's Davey I don't understand. After all this time . . . All he had to do was come to me. I gave him money before, whenever he needed it. And it was never like blackmail. It was like I said: a gift to a friend who did me a favor. We even joked once that I was paying him royalties, because I wrote "For Tonight" right after Lorraine's letter, inspired by all that crap about always and forever. Davey used to swear he made one chord change, but he didn't; it's all mine, just like the rest of the songs."

She set the guitar on the floor, its narrow neck leaning against the couch. I was afraid it would fall. "I don't understand him turning nasty like this," she said, and I'd never heard her sound so tired, so drained. "He knew Lorraine's death wasn't my fault. It happened, and maybe I should have handled things differently. If I had a moment to live over, that's the one I'd take."

"When you found Brenda dead, when you called me, you were talking about Lorraine, weren't you?"

"It was like a nightmare, like it was happening all over again. And that's when I knew Davey must have gone nuts, killing poor Brenda for no reason except to remind me that I owed him for keeping his mouth shut. That's when I decided I'd pay him, hock what I had, go into debt, take any contract MGA would give me, pay him, and get on with my life."

I picked up the guitar. The aged wood felt silky smooth. There was a deep scratch to the left of the pickguard. It smelled like old cigars. "Tell me more about Lorraine."

"What's to tell?" Dee said, head bowed. "I liked her. I cared about her."

"Do you think she was trying to kill you too? With the pills and the booze?"

"I don't think about it anymore. I don't think about anything but the music. The music, this goddamned ungrateful music is my fucking life, Carlotta. If I can't have the music,

I don't want anything else. I've given up what most people care about. I don't have a home. I don't have a kid. I was scared shitless the night Lorraine died. And I wasn't going to let Lorraine's death be what people thought about when they heard my name. Dee Willis. *Dee Willis*. People think about my songs when they hear my name. Not some ugly suicide from a long time ago . . .

"Oh, how could Davey do it?" she asked, shaking her head and holding out her hands as if they could wring an answer out of the air. "Why now? Why go to some goddamn lawyer? I thought if I found him, if you found him . . . Maybe he got so drunk, he was out of his mind — "

I plucked an A minor chord, followed by an E minor that seemed to hover in the air. "The blackmailer had to go through a lawyer," I said. "He couldn't come to you. He's not Davey."

"What?"

"He's not Davey," I repeated. "Davey's not blackmailing you. Davey talked too much to the wrong person. And that wasn't his fault either."

Dee ran her hands through her dark curls, squeezed them to her temples as if she had a killer headache. "Stop hitting minors, for chrissake," she said. "Tell me who the hell the blackmailer is. Tell me — am I better off than I thought? Or worse? What happens next?"

"Depends."

"On?"

"You. You can shut up and pay a fortune to the guy. And remember, he's not just a blackmailer either. Ray Daggett killed Brenda."

"Who?" Dee said. "Run that by me slow."

"Brenda's boyfriend. Brenda's 'boy-toy.' "

"Brenda's little honey? Ray? How's he know Davey? How's he know about Lorraine? I mean, maybe he killed Brenda 'cause they had some kind of lovers' shit, but I don't understand him blackmailing me."

"He knew Davey. I'll explain it all later, but the question you have to answer now is simple: Do you want him to go free?"

Dee dropped her hands to her lap, looked at me for a long time before answering. "Brenda was a tough cookie," she said finally. "We didn't agree on much. But she was a real decent player. The Reverend would have called her a 'sportin' ' player."

"I take it that means you don't think her killer should walk. Good. But you'll have to talk to that cop friend of mine. You'll have to tell him about Lorraine."

"Shit," Dee said. "Shit. I have to think. Either

give me back the guitar or play it, okay?"

My fingers found the notes to something the group used to sing. I was surprised I remembered the words.

> *"Look down the road, far as my*
> *eyes can see,*
> *Far as my eyes can see.*
> *I couldn't see nothing that looked*
> *like mine to me."*

"Nice," Dee said. "Skip James?"

I kept playing; not singing, just fooling around with the melody.

"You said you found Davey," Dee said. "I knew you could."

I sang another verse. "Yeah," I said.

She spoke softly over the guitar break. "Did you talk to him? Do you think he'd give me back Lorraine's letter?"

When I told her where he was, she started to cry. I didn't have the heart to ask her any more questions. I didn't really need to anyway.

CHAPTER THIRTY-SIX

Once she got her voice under control, Dee phoned Hal. I listened while she lied. She told him she had a twenty-four-hour bug, and wanted no one, absolutely no one, admitted to her room. No calls put through. I could hear his voice rise in panic over the receiver. She assured him that she'd be a hundred percent for the concert. He shouted that he needed to see her, that he'd be there right away, that he'd bring a doctor. She yelled him down, vetoing all suggestions. Then she hung up, put a hand to her stomach, and ran for the bathroom.

She was in there a long time. I could hear an occasional retching noise.

I used the interval to make a call of my own. Mooney agreed to meet us in the lobby.

When Dee ventured out, she seemed okay, her face washed pale, no makeup, wet washcloth to her mouth. I checked the medicine cabinet, the bathroom wastebasket, found nothing with which she could have done herself much harm.

"You scared, Dee?" I asked gently when I found her stretched lifelessly on the sofa.

"Of AIDS? Shit, I been tested so many times. Everybody in the business has, except the Singing Nun. I haven't got it. Not because I took such good care of myself and never screwed around with guys whose names I didn't know, and guys who shot drugs, and guys who slept with other guys. There's nothing wrong with me. I just feel rotten, rotten, rotten."

"Mooney, the cop I told you about, the one you met at the station, will be downstairs in ten minutes. You want him to come up here?"

"Here?" She stared at the elegant room as if it were a prison cell. "Shit, no. I need to get out. There's a bar in the lobby. We can have a drink."

"You could have one here. Room service."

"Hal told them to cut off the liquor supply. Nice, huh?"

"He can do that?"

"He pays the bills."

We had to wait until Mooney phoned up and called off the door guards. Dee spent most of the time in the bathroom, and when she emerged, she was subtly different. She still looked pale and sad, don't get me wrong, but she'd managed a faint radiant glow. A damn good makeup job. No blush, pale lipstick. Like a bride, I thought. Maybe the reason I can never figure Dee out is that part of her is always onstage.

Even if I hadn't known her for twelve years, I'd have been impressed by the way she handled herself in the lobby, by the way she tried to handle Mooney.

"Have you caught him yet?" she asked quickly, taking Mooney's hand and hanging on a little too long for a routine shake. "Brenda's boyfriend?"

To Mooney, the line must have read like overwhelming concern. To me, it seemed a calculated opener: if the cops have already caught the murderer, then I won't have to talk about Lorraine.

No such luck. No Ray, Mooney said.

We moved into the bar, which was really a lounge, full of linen-covered tables, potted palm trees, and gold-framed oil paintings of the Public Garden. The hostess tried to seat us near a window. Dee murmured something and we wound up at a table near the back of the room, secluded behind the greenery.

"Do you know where the bastard lives?" Dee asked as soon as she'd ordered a Scotch and soda. Mooney and I stuck to coffee.

"We've got an address, thanks to Carlotta. I took some troops out there. Seems like he moved the night Brenda died."

"Moved," Dee echoed.

I noticed the way her eyes never left Mooney's face, except to slip occasionally to his hands. Musicians are vain about their hands. I wondered if Mooney was.

"No forwarding address," Mooney said. "Scooted owing money to the landlord."

The waitress arranged Dee's drink on a coaster. Our coffee came in a large silver pot.

"Dammit," Dee said as soon as the waitress was out of earshot. She acknowledged my presence at the table, stared at me for a long time. I nodded encouragement.

She stared down at her hands, rock-steady on the glass, and said, "Brenda was killed to scare me, to send me a message."

"Do you want a lawyer present during this conversation, Miss Willis?" Mooney asked.

"No. No. Call me Dee, please. I'm not making any sort of confession here, any official statement, except — "

"It's the 'excepts' I worry about," Mooney said.

"Just listen," Dee said. "Please. I don't want any freaking lawyer. I just want to tell you the truth."

I'm not saying Dee lied. But the way she told the story to Mooney — well, the focus was slightly different. It was a miracle that she — Dee — had emerged alive from that harrowing night. It was no longer the story of Lorraine's declaration of love, its rejection, her suicide. It was Dee's tale, about Dee's terror, Dee's survival.

Mooney said, "So you figure Brenda's boyfriend knew the gist of it from what he overheard at the hospice, right? And he wanted to set the stage, show you he knew what happened at Lorraine's, so you'd better pay up or else."

Dee answered in a husky murmur, and I was aware of the power of that ever so controlled voice. "I don't see why he had to kill her. Just finding her drunk, or unconscious, would have sent me the same message."

"Did the two of you have a thing going? You and Brenda?" Mooney asked.

Dee didn't approve of his question. I did. Mooney was treating her like a suspect, not worshiping at her feet like one of her adoring fans.

"Does that matter?" she snapped. "I didn't kill her. And no, we did not have a 'thing' going."

I sipped at my coffee and said, "The way I read it, Brenda helped Ray out with the blackmail, only she didn't know it."

"How?" Mooney said.

I asked Dee, "Do you remember when Brenda started going with Ray?"

"It was one quick pick-up, let me tell you. Guy made the play for her, sent her flowers, said he'd loved listening to her with Silverhawk, her last group. Brenda — well, she was flattered. Who the hell wouldn't be? The guys in the band all have young chickies who wait at the hotels, hoping some guy who can play a C chord will give them a toss. It's a little different for women on the road. Some women, anyway. Brenda didn't have a guy in every port. She's getting — she was getting older. A young lover's not bad for the road."

Mooney raised an eyebrow.

I said, "Stuart Lockwood claims he turned Ray — that's Ray pretending to be Davey — down the first time he came to the office because Ray hadn't brought any proof. So Ray goes to work. First he steals old pictures of Dee from Davey. But that's not enough, so he makes a play for Brenda. Once she's hooked, he hands her a line: I'm such a fan, maybe you could give me your sheet music to copy? Or maybe he asked her to get him the originals. It would be easy to come up with a story: I'm broke, and some collector will pay big bucks for the original transcription. Maybe he just stole her sheet music and to hell with finesse. He didn't know music; he never figured Brenda would just have the bass line."

"Wait up," Mooney said. "Why didn't he steal the music from Davey? If he could rip off all this other stuff? Why'd he need Brenda at all?"

Dee signaled the waitress for a second drink and said, "I can tell you that: Davey wouldn't have music. He couldn't read music. He could play like an angel, back you on any song in any key — but he never learned to read."

Mooney sighed. "Three hundred thousand dollars. People have done stranger things to get it."

"If he'd asked for a thousand, forged Davey's name to a note, I'd have paid, no questions asked," Dee said.

"See, Mooney," I said. "That's the whole thing. Ray went for too much. Davey — Davey's sickness — must have talked the money angle way up. He's in and out. Sometimes he makes sense; sometimes he doesn't. Maybe he really believes, sometimes, that he wrote part of 'For Tonight,' or maybe he believes Dee owes him the royalties for that song because she wrote it about Lorraine, and he kept quiet about Lorraine. And Ray listens to him babble and figures Dee for the perfect golden goose. Brenda must have realized something was going on. Maybe Ray was too insistent about the music, maybe she noticed how jumpy Dee was getting."

"So she asked the boyfriend what it was really all about," Mooney said.

"She could have suspected the sudden come-on. She asked a question too many, that's for sure. Maybe she threatened to tell Dee she'd given Ray some music. That alone would have started Dee thinking, maybe ruined the whole plan. If Dee even suspected it wasn't really Davey demanding the money, no way she'd pay, right? I mean, Ray can't exactly stand up in court and give evidence about Lorraine's death, no matter what he might have overheard at the hospital. It's not only hearsay, it's hearsay from Davey, and a dozen doctors will testify that Davey is out of it most of the time, with AIDS-related dementia, or drug-induced hallucinations. Ray had to go through a lawyer, through some kind of go-between. Hell, have you seen him? He looks like he was in diapers when Dee wrote 'For Tonight.' "

"I've seen his mug shot," Mooney said.

"Not a citizen?" I asked.

"Amazing he had gainful employment. Must have lied on his application, unless the hospital's big on taking Deer Island alumni. Saint John's is probably missing half its equipment."

I said, "He ever work in a hotel?"

"I can run ,a check," Mooney said. "He

could have killed Brenda in her own room and moved her to Dee's with a maid's cart. Remade the bed in Brenda's room with linen off the cart and stuffed the dirty sheets into a laundry bag. He was an orderly, right? So even if he didn't do hotel stuff, he'd be able to make a bed."

I said, "Remember the two circles on the magazine cover, two drinks, but just one glass? I think he got Brenda started in her own room, maybe fed her most of the booze and pills there, made the mess there, cleaned up there, like you said. Brenda was probably pretty pissed off at Dee; Dee had yelled at her during rehearsal. So Ray says something like, let's go see the bitch, and half carries Brenda down the hall. Who's gonna see them in the middle of the night? And if somebody sees them, he can change his plans. Maybe he knew Dee was out; maybe he figured he'd leave Brenda's body in the living room if Dee was asleep in the bedroom. We can assume he got a key from a desk clerk; it wouldn't have been hard. Dee's not in, so he says to Brenda, let's do it in her bed, show the bitch what we think of her. And he keeps feeding Brenda pills, giving her booze, till she passes out."

"I'll buy it," Mooney said. "And he'd have the syringe for the finishing touch. Two birds, one stone. Get Brenda out of the way. Scare Dee."

Dee's second drink arrived. She moistened her lips, said, mainly to me, "Then you don't think Ray snatched Lorraine's suicide note when he was stealing Davey's stuff?"

I said, "Come on, Dee. If he had it, if it reads as ugly as you say it does, he'd have made a direct approach, tried to sell it to you. Davey probably destroyed it years ago. He loved you, Dee. Lorraine loved you. Hell, we all loved you. Cal, the whole damn group, I suppose. Isn't that what you want? For everybody to freaking love you?"

I kept my voice low. Both Mooney and Dee pretended they hadn't heard my outburst.

A young man wearing a suit, a tie, and an overeager grin approached our table. "Excuse me," he said, "but aren't you Dee Willis?"

"I'm going up to the room," she said abruptly, finishing her drink in a single gulp. "No, mister, I'm not. You made a mistake."

CHAPTER
THIRTY-SEVEN

I glanced up and saw Roz waving at me from an alcove behind a palm. I almost choked on my coffee.

"Can you wait a minute, Mooney?" I said calmly, glad he was carefully eyeing Dee's departure, making sure she headed straight for the elevators. "I need to hit the bathroom."

"I'll dial upstairs," he said. "Meet you back here."

A waitress pointed me in the direction of a small hallway. The ladies' room had three stalls, three complete bathrooms, really, each with its own sink, so you wouldn't have to wash up in semipublic view. Roz joined me while I was drying my hands on an individually rolled towel I'd taken from a decorative basket. No brown paper towels from a dispenser here.

For her role as undercover groupie, Roz had dyed her hair the color of red licorice, then cornrowed a small section near her right temple. The corresponding section at the left temple, crimped and puffed, looked like some exotic foodstuff, not hair. Starting from the bottom she wore black boots, ultra-tight shiny black stirrup pants, and one of her most prized T-shirts, a souvenir of a trip to New Orleans. Purple, with a row of oysters across her more than ample breasts. Beneath them, three lines of print said it all:

"Shuck me, suck me, eat me raw."

Just the tone the manager sought to cultivate in her hotel. I could imagine her urgent memo to her supervisor: No more rock groups. No more blues groups. No more music groups. Perhaps a dispensation could be considered for the Vienna Boys Choir.

"Subtle," I said to Roz, as we exchanged glances in the mirror.

"I didn't know groupies went for subtle," she said while applying lipstick to a mouth that could hardly have been redder. "And I haven't even met a guy I'd like to shake hands with, anyway. The drummer's strictly off-limits, according to Mimi. The keyboard man's so drugged out he hasn't gotten it up in years, also according to Mimi. The lead guitar's a hunk-and-a-half, but he's so stuck on himself he probably does it with mirrors."

"Cut to the good part, Roz. Mimi may decide to visit the little girls' room."

"There aren't a whole lot of good parts," Roz said. "Little bitch doesn't want a sister or a best girlfriend, that's for sure. I'm the competition."

"So what have you got?"

"For starters, Mimi is not Mimi. Try Matilda Hooper. Honest. I borrowed her wallet. I'll bet my T-shirt she has a rap sheet, but it's probably a sealed juvie. Fifteen, she says, but I'd make it seventeen. Been on the scene since she was ten, but I think most of what she says she makes up on the spot. She brags about dealing drugs, using drugs, doing guys, doing break-ins. If she does half what she says, she's gonna be dead by the time she's twenty."

"She do our break-in?"

"She was busy that night, and she giggled when she said busy. If she was having sex with one of the guys in the band, one of the techies, one of the roadies, she'd have told every detail, no giggles. Sex with musicians — that's, like, her business. She keeps their names written down in a book."

"What else?"

"Look, this isn't working out real well. Mimi seems to hate my guts. What I've told you is everything I've managed to wedge out of her, and everything I'm likely to get. I bought her drinks, the whole bit, but she's gonna just pass out if I keep it up."

"Has she said anything about Hal?"

"She thinks he's pretty cute for an old guy. That's all she said, but you want an impression, I'll give you one. I think she's close to him. He's the road manager. He provides access to the stars."

"She sleep with him?"

"Doesn't brag about it. She once licked Mick Jagger's right nipple. That she brags about."

"Freddie bring in the drugs, or Mimi?"

"Not sure, but I'd say Mimi. Maybe both. You like my hair like this?"

"Awesome."

She was accenting her eyelids with a substance that looked like a cross between glitter and clown makeup.

"I'm really picking up some fashion tips. You got to swing with a younger crowd, I guess," she said.

I'm never sure when Roz is joking. I left it alone. "So you figure you're finished as a groupie?" I said.

"Mimi's gonna have some goon beat me up if I stick around," Roz said. "That's what I think."

"So quit," I said. "Go to the library. Do a periodical check. I'm not sure if the BPL collects stuff like *Guitar* magazine, but maybe they do. See what you can pick up about Hal

Grady. Like what groups he's managed. I think Mimi said one was called the Bow-Wows — "

"They weren't bad," Roz said. "I heard they made big bucks on tour, but their album went nowhere."

"A road band," I murmured. I started washing my hands all over again.

"What's that mean?" Roz asked. "What are you thinking?"

I said, "Some bands, they're great live; make a lot of money on tour. Exciting show. Good-looking players. Some bands are studio bands. Close harmony, special effects. They score big on album sales. Very few groups do both."

"So?"

"I was wondering whether Hal specializes in road bands, bands that do a whole lot better on ticket sales than they do on albums, tapes, CD's, what have you. Like the Bow-Wows."

"Would that be unusual?" Roz asked.

"It would sure be interesting," I said. "Check it out, if you can. The bands Hal's managed, see if they all happen to be money-making road bands and studio zeroes. You know where to look?"

"Everyplace from *Variety* on down, I suppose."

"Good," I said. "And you can always ask

a librarian, if they talk to people who wear obscene T-shirts."

"Tell me the truth," she said. "You think I should leave my hair like this?"

CHAPTER THIRTY-EIGHT

Mooney had finished his coffee by the time I got back to the table. "This stuff makes me jumpy," he said. "Or maybe you make me jumpy. Why do I have the feeling you're holding something back?"

"Because I am," I said flatly. "But before we talk about it, I want to know what's gonna happen." I nodded in the direction of the elevators in case he didn't catch my drift.

"To Dee Willis? Nothing. Nobody's gonna bring up that old suicide. Christ, the guys at Jamaica Plain are bitching about me having the nerve to even ask for the file on that one. Say they can't find it; it's in some warehouse. I can fill out a form and maybe they can get it to me in six to ten weeks, if anybody ever bothered with the paperwork."

"Cooperative," I said. "I thought suicide was still a crime in this state."

"They are cooperative," Mooney said defensively. "They're also overworked. Look, nobody's ever gonna know if the girl was dead or alive when Dee left. Nobody's ever gonna know if your friend could have been saved. I mean, let's say she might have been barely alive. Maybe if Dee had called the cops, the paramedics, somebody, this Lorraine might have stayed in a coma for the rest of her life, another Karen Quinlan. What I mean is, maybe Dee did her a favor by walking out. You were the dead girl's friend, right? Does it make a difference to you? Do you think I should rake it all up again? You think this Lorraine's parents want to hear that maybe their daughter didn't just kill herself, maybe she tried to take Dee Willis along for the ride?"

"That's Dee's story," I said.

"The corpse ain't talking," Mooney replied. "You think the parents really want to know their little girl slept with other little girls? How come you didn't know that? Being her friend and all?"

"Tell me about it, Mooney," I said angrily. "You know all the gay guys in the squad room? You can pick 'em out? All I know is she never came on to me. Neither did Dee. I must not be her type."

Mooney said, "I don't plan to call a news conference and neither do you. Let it lie. Let the people who can sleep nights sleep."

"And Ray?"

"We've got a warrant, and we'll keep looking till we find him. Sooner or later, unless he's smarter than the average killer, he's gonna show up at his sister's house, go see an old girlfriend or some cousin in New Bedford, and we'll nail him."

"You don't think Dee's in any danger?"

"From him? I think he wants money, pure and simple. If he's real dumb, he'll get in touch with Lockwood, and from what I understand the lawyer will roll him over."

"He killed somebody. He might figure he's got nothing to lose."

"There hasn't been any public outcry about Brenda's death. One more musician suicide doesn't rate newsprint, unless the victim's a star. Still, if you want to beef up security around the concert, we can do that, a little."

"And I can ask her road manager to add some bodyguards," I said slowly. "On second thought, maybe arrange something myself." I wondered if Gloria's big brothers might like a chance to earn some of MGA/America's money.

"Now," Mooney said, "you want to tell me the rest? Like what Roz is dressed up to be?"

"You saw her?"

"I'm not blind, Carlotta."

"I thought you were fully occupied watching Dee swing her butt."

"My, my, that lady does attract vipers to

her camp," Mooney said, shaking his head at me.

"Maybe it takes one to attract them," I said. "You want to hear about the others?"

"Like who?"

"Like who stole my handbag."

"Ray, right?"

"Uh-uh. Ray has been a very careful guy. He's been working as an orderly, listening to Davey for months; he's been cool. And I know he didn't trash my house."

"So who did?"

"That's where Roz comes in. She's researching the situation."

"In that getup?"

"Of course, you could do it better, but then you'd say I was using the department's resources to do my own work."

"Does it have anything to do with Mickey Manganero?"

"It does."

"Drug enforcement drools when they hear his name," Mooney said. "And the Boston Police are, of course, interested in helping out DEA."

"Want to go to a concert with me?" I asked. "It's a hard ticket to come by, but I've got a friend."

"Two tickets? Just you and me? Like a date?"

"Three tickets," I said, "and a chance to earn major points with a cooperating law enforcement agency. You get to invite a colleague from DEA."

"Sounds okay," Mooney said cautiously.

"Pick somebody who likes music," I said, and then I told him what I knew about Hal Grady — that he gambled, that he'd recommended a local loan shark to Dee Willis, that Dee had mentioned Hal's particular fondness for Atlantic City, Manganero's old stomping ground. I asked him if he had ways to find out whether Hal Grady was handling more cash than he ought to be.

"You think Manganero's using Grady to launder money?"

"Offhand I can think of half a dozen ways to do it, and I'm not even a crook. Say Hal's touring a real dog band, low ticket sales. Well, he gives away big blocks of tickets — to hospitals, charity groups, fills the house. I think they call it 'papering' the house. The auditorium's full, but there's not much money in the till. Grady gets the extra cash from Manganero."

"Another way?" Mooney asked.

"On a tour like this one, a guaranteed sellout, Hal can cook the books. Top tickets for this show are a little under thirty bucks. When Hal writes it up, he adds ten bucks a ticket.

The extra comes from Manganero. Or Grady can lie about the size of the house. You think somebody goes through the books and wonders whether some stadium really holds forty-two thousand seven hundred and sixty-two seats? Or he could jiggle the number of premium seats. You know, a place like the Performance Center, they must have different prices for orchestra seats and balcony seats. Hal doubles the number of expensive seats, halves the number of cheapies."

"That's only four ways," Mooney said, deadpan.

"Use your imagination," I said.

"If Hal's reporting a bigger take than he should for a sellout, you'd think somebody at MGA would notice," Mooney said.

"So the Gianellis have got somebody at MGA, or maybe somebody at the bank. Maybe both. You find that hard to believe?"

"No."

"They've probably got the police commissioner."

"Can you back that up?"

"No, Mooney, I can't. I'm just getting a little carried away here. All I want to say is there are a lot of ways that Manganero can use a guy like Hal Grady."

"You think somebody from MGA is involved?"

"If Hal's been doing a lot of work for MGA, I'd say that's a definite possibility."

"Think Dee knows about it?"

I shrugged my shoulders and sipped coffee, not really tasting it. "At long last, I think I can say I've learned something about Dee," I ventured after a long pause. "There's probably nothing she wouldn't do to get ahead."

"Try this one. Do you believe the story she told me?"

"About Lorraine?"

"Yeah."

"Like you said, after all these years, does it make a difference? Is it gonna make Lorraine any less dead?"

Mooney said, "Did this Lorraine maybe write the songs?"

"Shit, Mooney," I said, "no. You've got a mind like a cop, a damned devious mind. No!"

"Why so fierce?" Mooney's voice was soft.

"No," I repeated. "Absolutely no."

CHAPTER THIRTY-NINE

When Mooney realized where our seats were — top row, upper balcony, on the aisle — he gave me a long look. "Thought you had a friend," he said.

I scooted into the row, leaving him to follow. The other man, Mooney's choice from DEA, a hawk-nosed, unsmiling type, sank into the aisle seat with a grunt.

The steep angle made our seats seem so high that I felt like I might need an oxygen mask, feared that if I fell, I'd slide straight down to the orchestra pit. But when the houselights dimmed, the movement and the music and the spotlights melded in a way they hadn't from the fourth row. The stage looked like a jeweled miniature, the showpiece of a museum collection.

I glanced at my watch and hoped the dismal warm-up band — a two-girl, two-boy, no-harmony disaster — would keep to its allotted half hour. I doubted anyone would beg for an encore. I was right.

Dee entered to a roar like thunder, in her

shimmery white tux, rhinestone earrings dangling to her shoulders. She muttered a brief thank you, tapped her high-heeled foot, yelled "six, seven, eight" over the crowd's salute, and opened with "Steel Guitar."

I closed my eyes and remembered how it felt to be part of the music. I play alone now. I never tried another group after Lorraine died, after Cal left. The only group thing I do now is volleyball, and when the game's just right, when every player is in sync, when the ball floats over the net in sweet slow-motion, and you know just where you're going to hit it, and just how the opposing player will respond, there's a touch of the magic.

But volleyball's a cheap trick compared to playing behind somebody like Dee, next to Cal, hearing your own sound join other sounds, become something better, something greater. I remembered moments of perfect silence at a song's end, followed by the longing for one more verse, one more chorus, five more minutes of that close, aching harmony, soul to soul, like sex, like sorcery.

For an instant of pure hatred, I wished I could somehow prove that Dee had killed Lorraine. She'd have done it, if Lorraine had stood in her way. Not provided the pills, not urged the drink. But walked away, walked away from what might have been pure gesture, pure drama, on Lorraine's part. *I love you. If you leave me, I will kill myself. I swear I will.* I could almost hear the words in Lorraine's clear, soft voice.

I considered my years of guilt — over Lorraine, over Cal. I'd misunderstood Lorraine; I'd driven Cal away. That's what I'd thought. But Dee had taken Lorraine. Dee had taken Cal. Taken everything she ever wanted.

She started to sing again, and the hatred faded like summer mist. Dee was right. I couldn't tell the singer from the song.

I glanced at Mooney to see if Dee's witchcraft had touched him. He was staring at his wristwatch, on the job. The DEA man on the aisle, I swear, was wearing earplugs.

Freddie on drums, Ron on lead guitar, the keyboard man, a new skinny bass, all faded into the background as Dee took hold of the audience and sang. I might have searched her face for signs of turmoil if I could have seen it without opera glasses. I was glad I didn't have any. I knew what I'd see. The same look Cal had on his face when he played. Dee alone with her music.

The crowd was ecstatic — diehard fans, the old Boston bar crowd, welcoming their bigtime star home. They gave her an ovation after every number. I tried to join in and found

I could barely clap my hands together with a hollow echo.

She didn't say anything between songs, just dropped her dark head until the music started up again, pumping new life into her, as if she were a doll, a puppet energized by the songs.

"There's a train every day, leaving either way," she sang. I wondered if she'd chosen her set for me, or for Davey. Most likely Jimmy Ranger had lined up the songs he considered the most solidly commercial. Anything else was sentimental crap, I reminded myself. Dee was an industry, not a simple country girl singing the blues.

She owned that stage; it was her real estate. She strutted and sang, danced when the music moved her. From the balcony, she was the most beautiful woman imaginable. She'd have to be, with that voice. Only during the applause did she let go of the illusion, and in between the seventh and eighth songs, after a muttered "thank you," she said clearly, "This one's for Davey."

It was "For Tonight." She'd been singing for forty-five minutes. I elbowed Mooney. It was time for us to go.

CHAPTER FORTY

No one noticed when we left. That was the idea behind top-row aisle seats. I led the way to the little room Hal Grady used as an office. The night's standing-room-only haul wouldn't begin its journey to the deposit vault next door till midnight.

That's what Hal had sworn when DEA, on Mooney's advice, had picked up Dee's "gamblin' man" that afternoon. It was, Mooney told me, a long and interesting conference. Confronted with salary records and bank account statements — items difficult to reconcile — Grady had at first attributed his fortune to gambling luck. Mooney told me he thought Hal would demand a lawyer at that point. But threatened with the IRS, he became eager to cooperate, increasingly eager for a chance to stay out of jail. Eager to the point of agreeing to wear a DEA wire tonight.

I wondered if Mickey Manganero, years earlier, had seen the long-term money-laundering potential in Hal's career, sought him out in Atlantic City with attractive terms. I wondered if any of the faceless MGA execs had been bought or threatened by the

Gianellis. Grady swore his only contact was Manganero.

According to Hal, tradition dictated that two security guards would walk the money to the bank, one being George Wolfe, with an *e*, the man on the exempt list. The other was generally somebody burly enough to discourage neighborhood punks. Tonight it would be Leroy, Gloria's youngest brother. He's not the largest of the trio, but he's the meanest, the one you'd least like to meet in a dark alley.

As we walked, the hawk-nosed man from DEA spoke quietly into what seemed to be an ordinary shirt-collar button. The Drug Enforcement Agency always has the latest in high-tech chic.

They'd had an interest in Big Mickey long before I'd had my first chat with Joanne Triola. The guy with Mooney and me, an old DEA hand, stared at the two of us with the burnt-out expression of a man with a hopeless job, pried what I'd mistaken for ordinary earplugs out of his ears, and said, "The wire's working, everything's going great." He tried to summon enthusiasm, but his tone said: I can't believe something won't go wrong at the last minute.

A burnout case for sure.

"Want to listen?" he said to me.

Dee's wailing voice was faint in the background. Mainly I could hear Freddie's thumping drums. I said, "Okay."

He passed over a plug and I stuck it in my right ear. It wasn't high-quality sound, but I could make out the words. Hal sounded nervous.

"Look," I heard him blurt suddenly, "I don't wanna do this stuff anymore, understand?"

"You haven't got a lot of choices, Hal buddy." Manganero's voice was deep and pleasant, relaxed. I remembered him resplendent in his dinner jacket at the MGA/America bash, where his only mistake had been to chat with Sam Gianelli's girlfriend. Sam didn't exactly advertise my career to his dad's business associates.

"The money's good," Manganero continued. "Keeps your kid in that fancy school, right? You know, lots of things happen to kids away at school, teenage girls, especially."

"Bastard," I muttered, under my breath.

Mr. DEA spoke into his button. "We got enough? You sure the tape's good?"

"Take him," came the response, loud enough to make me yank the plug out of my ear and hold it gingerly an inch away. Two agents appeared on either side of the office door, armed with 9mm automatics, wearing bulletproof vests with DEA stenciled back and front, the better to avoid shooting each other.

I moved aside, a habit of mine when the firepower index is high. I wasn't there for any gunplay; I was there for the next step, the walk to George Wolfe's office, to keep Hal's morale up — more to the point, to make sure he didn't take it into his head to skip.

DEA didn't like it. Mooney wasn't fond of the arrangement either. But Hal had insisted on my company. During his DEA session, he'd volunteered the opinion that nobody would mistake me for a cop.

To ensure that nobody would, I'd dressed for the concert, or rather the party after the concert, with more than usual care. Tight black jeans that really didn't look like jeans, a green silk blouse that made my eyes seem emerald. I wore Aunt Bea's gold locket in the low-cut V-neck.

Manganero stuck his hands in the air and kept his lips clamped when DEA busted the door. He was so quiet I wondered if he was automatically considering the possibility of a wire. The bills stacked on Hal's desk hadn't come from any ticket sales. But entered into the Bank of Commerce through Hal's tricky bookkeeping, with George Wolfe's help — for which he would earn a couple thousand off the top — the money would lose its identity until the time came for it to enter a seemingly "legit" Gianelli-run business.

Green & White Cab is not one of them. Or so Sam says.

The DEA agents hurriedly photographed Manganero's banded stacks of bills, concentrating on serial numbers to establish a direct chain of evidence, counting the cash. They hoped to trace it further down the pipeline, to whichever MGA executive had been bought or coerced into involvement, whichever bank manager had been suborned. The same signature on a series of checks made out to a Gianelli front for, say, nine thousand, nine hundred-odd dollars would be of great interest to DEA.

Hal murmured nervously, "They'll be waiting for me."

Manganero, handcuffed, shot him a glance that could have fried fish. He hadn't been certain about the wire; now he was.

"They'll wait a little longer, Hal," Mooney said soothingly. "Don't freak on us now."

"It's just . . . I'm having trouble — "

"Take a deep breath," I counseled. "Another one."

"It's just, it all catches up to you," Hal said with a bewildered shrug.

I thought about Dee. "Sometimes yes, sometimes no," I said.

"Believe me," he said, as if he knew who

I was thinking about, "I never would've made trouble for Dee. I love that girl. She should've kicked me out the first time I tried to borrow money to make up a bad debt. In a way, she kept me in the business. And now I'm in way over my head."

"Mimi did the really dumb thing," I said.

"Little bitch," he agreed, without anger. "She's Manganero's little piece, when she's not spreading it around. And, like the jerk I am, I had to confide in her, tell her I was worried about you."

"You didn't buy it when Dee said I was a friend?"

"I figured maybe you could be a replacement for Brenda. Maybe Dee was looking to shake up the band. But Mimi said Dee talked about some license you had. I wanted to have a look at that."

"So you arranged to have somebody steal my purse."

"Yeah, I did that, but I didn't expect any knifeplay, and the break-in was Mimi's idea of a night out. I didn't even know about it till she told me."

The DEA had finished with the money. Hawk-nose said, "Look, Hal, why don't I take the walk with you?"

"No," Hal said stubbornly. "That's not the deal I made. Me and her. She can go right into the office with me. You can't."

We walked slowly. Hal seemed to need to talk, wire or no wire. It was so simple to slip into it, he said. The money stuff. He knew it was wrong, but it was so damned simple.

I agreed. It's easy to buy people, especially with the carrot-and-stick approach favored by the Manganeros of the world. Either you help me launder this money and earn a nice chunk of change for yourself, or your fifteen-year-old daughter has a very unpleasant experience.

We heard a loud burst of applause signaling the end of a number, and Hal stood up to his full five-five, as proud of Dee as any parent.

I whispered, "Turn off the mike for a second, Hal."

"Huh?"

"You heard me."

He undid a couple of shirt buttons, rotated a dial. "What?" he said. "The guys are gonna be pissed."

"Tell me once, tell me the truth, did Dee know about the money laundering?"

"No," he said.

"The truth, Hal," I said. "Between you and me."

He looked at me for a long time. Then he said quietly, "No way. Swear on my mother's grave. Can I turn it back on now?"

"Wait. Did Dee ever talk about Lorraine Holbrook? Ever say she learned any song from somebody named Lorraine?"

"Sorry," Hal said, staring at the floor. "I don't think she ever mentioned the name. I'm turning the mike back on now, okay? I don't want these guys to think I'm crossing them. I've got enough trouble."

We knocked at George's locked door — three-two-three — as Hal had arranged. A tense voice ordered us to come in and close the door. Hal, hastily buttoning his shirt, maybe envisioning his future in the Federal Witness Protection Program, didn't notice anything wrong.

CHAPTER FORTY-ONE

"Lock it behind you," the slender man in the security guard uniform barked.

I heard the click as Hal obeyed. Hal was still wearing the wire, I reminded myself, sucking in a deep breath. But had he turned it back to the proper volume? Was anybody tuned in? Were the DEA listeners partying in their van, celebrating the capture of Manganero?

This was the simple part, after all.

DEA agents would pick up George, along with Gloria's brother Leroy, as soon as they left the building, and tail them to the bank. What could go wrong before then? DEA hadn't even sent an agent with me, figuring a judge would like it better if an independent citizen could back up Hal's statement and testify that Manganero's dubious cash had mingled with legitimate concert receipts in George's office.

Hal introduced me to George, the man on the bank's exempt list, a heavyset middle-aged fellow who didn't say anything beyond hello.

I managed a smile. Maybe George didn't realize anything was wrong either. Hal hadn't noticed. That left me, and I'd seen the smudgy-eyed man only once. Was I absolutely certain? I hadn't even asked Mooney for a peek at his mug shot.

"You think the two of you can handle this?" I said, giggling in a way I never do, speaking too loudly, trying to catch the ear of some quick-witted technician in the sound van. "Hell of a lot of money. Must weigh a ton."

George tried a weak laugh and said, "Yeah, they sent me a pint-sized assistant this week. Regular guy's off, uh, sick."

"Man your size doing security work," I said in a flirty voice. "You carry a big gun?"

"What's it to you?" Ray said. I took that for a yes, and hoped the DEA had picked it up.

How had Ray put Leroy out of commission? I prayed he'd used his brain and not his gun, envisioned a furious Leroy locked in some closet. How could I face Gloria if anything happened to brother Leroy? One thing: Ray hadn't stolen Leroy's clothes. The blue uniform fit his narrow frame precisely.

Christ, this guy was resourceful. If he couldn't get the money one way, he'd get it another.

"Who are you?" Ray addressed me warily.

"She's my baby tonight," Hal said cheerfully, slipping an arm around my waist, keeping to our cover story. "I like 'em tall."

I deviated from it. "I'm Dee's good buddy," I announced. "Dee and Mooney want to make sure every little nickel gets to the nest." I tried to sound as if I'd had a drink too many, slurring an occasional word. I listened, hoping for footsteps in the hall, on the stairs. Nothing.

George glanced at Hal's heavy satchel. "What's the count?"

While they shifted stacks of bills, I took a good look around the office. No other entrances or exits, not even a window. I memorized a poster of an early Crosby, Stills, Nash, and Young tour, stuck to one of the yellowed walls with pushpins. A bulletin board covered with pastel flyers announced upcoming events. A round schoolroom clock ticked. Eleven forty-six. Eleven forty-seven. I gave Ray a sidelong glance, wondering if the gun was in the back of his pants, tucked in his waistband, or in his side pocket. I couldn't spot a bulge.

"What're you staring at, bitch?"

"What do you think?"

"Hey," Hal said. "None of that talk."

I measured the distance between the desk and the door, between Ray and George. Could I stop him?

She was a decent player. That's what Dee

had said about Brenda. A tough cookie, and a decent player. Not a bad thing to have carved on your tombstone.

"Wait a minute," I said with a wide smile. "Haven't I seen you around? You a musician? No, don't tell me. Didn't I see you with what's-her-name? Brenda, Dee's bass player?"

There. I'd said it. Now would somebody in the damned sound truck clue Mooney that something weird was happening in the office where the nicely photographed money was about to slip into the wrong hands?

"Not me," Ray said curtly, quietly. I wondered if he remembered me from our brief encounter in Dee's suite.

"I guess everybody has a double," I said lightly. "But you sure look like Ray — Brenda's boyfriend, Ray. Hal, honey, do you believe everybody's got a double someplace?"

"I'm a security guard," Ray said firmly. "Shut up. Come on, George, let's go."

The money had been transferred to four canvas sacks, each zipped and padlocked. Reluctantly, George handed the small brass key to Ray.

Hal caught on at just the wrong time. He stared at the slight, dark-eyed man, and an uncertain smile flickered across his face. "Shit," he said, "you're no security guard, son. You don't have the build for it."

Then Hal turned to face me, as if the break in routine was my fault, cooked up by yours truly in conjunction with the Boston Police and the Drug Enforcement Agency. "What the hell is that son of a bitch doing here?" he demanded.

"Just give him the money, Hal," George urged, wiping a hand across his mouth. "He's got a freaking gun, okay? You just hand him the money. That's what we're supposed to do. It isn't your money; it isn't mine. It's not worth — "

Hal shook his head in disbelief as he listened. Then a grin spread slowly across his face and he interrupted. "Oh, kid," he said in a sorrowful voice, "have you ever fucked up." And he reached inside his shirt to show Ray the wire.

"Asshole," Ray screamed, pulling his gun, "I only want the goddamned money! What's it to you?"

"Don't!" I yelled at the same time.

I tried to shove Hal aside. The office was too small.

Ray shot him. Must have thought he was reaching for a gun.

I hit the floor before the explosion quit reverberating. To minimize myself as a target, to stay as low as possible in the tiny space,

I had to spread my legs and bend them at the knee like I was in the middle of a frog kick. My feet pressed against the wall. I could see one of Ray's shoes through the kneehole of the desk. Before he could fire again, I straightened both legs abruptly, shoving myself across the linoleum, grabbing his foot in both hands, and yanking it out from under him. George, fast for his size, thank God, smashed Ray's wrist with the edge of his hand and grabbed the little .22.

Hal was moaning on the floor.

I ripped open his shirt and yelled into the mike, "Get an ambulance up here, for chrissake! What the fuck are you guys doing?"

They were listening to the concert, the DEA man told me later. They were having trouble with the wire; its sound level had suddenly diminished. I didn't enlighten them, didn't tell them I'd asked Hal to turn it off. While they were yelling and blaming each other, I breathed into Hal's mouth, forcing his chest up and down, up and down. I thought he was alive when the paramedics took him.

He died at the hospital, Mooney told me. I didn't go to the party. My green silk shirt was covered with blood. I threw it in the trash when I got home.

I wondered whether I'd remember to add the price of the shirt to MGA/America's bill.

CHAPTER FORTY-TWO

I went to visit Davey at St. John's the next morning. I told Mooney where he could find me if he wanted to try.

I located my car in the lot, a red parking ticket gracing the driver's window. The Hummingbird, in its hardshell case, was shoved under Davey's mechanical bed.

"Has he seen it?" I asked Dr. Sanderley.

"Yes," he said with a brief, sad smile, and hurried off.

Davey's sunken eyes looked at me blankly.

"Who am I?" I asked.

"Dee?" he said, clearly uncertain.

"Never mind."

I slid the case out from under the bed and opened it.

I brushed a G chord, adjusted the E string. Played a few more chords, picked some notes, had to tune again. The strings sounded bright, acted new. I wondered if Cal had replaced them. A spare set of GHS strings nested in the velvet lining of the case. I'd brought my own picks.

I played the instrumentals first. Gary Davis's songs, old Baptist hymns, fiddle tunes, "Mole's Moan." I didn't trust my voice. Then, when I saw that Davey seemed to appreciate the music, I sang softly, Robert Johnson stuff, Blind Willie McTell.

Gloria's brother Leroy was okay; that was one bright spot. He'd been tripped, shoved down a flight of steps, and trussed like a turkey. He described it as the meanest clip he'd gotten since retiring from pro ball.

The DEA's case against Mickey Manganero was blown like smoke. No Hal to testify. Mimi would probably have her day in court, but not in the immediate future. If Roz's prediction held, maybe she wouldn't live to see it.

Roz had dyed her hair a curious shade of copper.

Stuart Lockwood had refused Ray's case. It would be assigned to a public defender. Nobody had figured out who Manganero's contact was among MGA's top brass. DEA was willing to wait for him to start signing checks.

Whoever it was, it wouldn't affect Dee. Nothing did.

I started a twelve-bar blues, so old it's labeled traditional; nobody knows who wrote the lines.

*"I'm goin' away, babe, I won't be
back 'til fall.
If I find me a new man, I won't be
back at all."*

I didn't hear the door open, but other voices joined in. I held the melody line, letting the others harmonize.

"Nice," a familiar alto murmured at the end.

I said, "Davey, Dee's come to say hello."

The roommate stared till his eyes bugged out.

I tried to hand off the guitar to Dee, but she'd brought Miss Gibson. Cal had brought a mandolin, a banjo, a bass. If it's got strings he can play it. The three of us sang and played till I was hoarse, till my calluses blistered and bled.

"I thought you'd be in Baltimore," I said to Dee.

"Postponed the show, the whole tour. We need a new road manager, a new bass." She gave a sidelong glance at Cal.

Davey faded in and out. Sometimes he'd close his eyes and we could only tell he was awake by the rhythmic tapping of a finger on the blanket. Sometimes he'd hold one of the instruments, his skeletal hands barely able to sound a note. He couldn't remember who we were, but his long-term memory seemed fine, so we played the old songs, and a few times he tried to join in with his ruined raspy voice.

"I was born in Tennessee,
I miss my friends and they miss me."

That's where I lost it. I set the guitar down carefully by the side of the bed and walked out.

Dee and Cal stayed. I hope they work it out. I hope he joins her tour, gets his music back.

I ripped the ticket off my window and shredded it without remorse, scattering the bits over the parking lot. Then I opened the door with my spare key, and retrieved the other from the dash. I planned to drive, drive all day, all night, all the next morning, until I found a bright yellow kite, a kite with a young Hispanic girl hanging on to the string.

I'm good at missing persons.

The employees of THORNDIKE PRESS hope you have enjoyed this Large Print book. All our Large Print titles are designed for easy reading, and all our books are made to last. Other Thorndike Large Print books are available at your library, through selected bookstores, or directly from us. For more information about current and upcoming titles, please call or mail your name and address to:

THORNDIKE PRESS
PO Box 159
Thorndike, Maine 04986
800/223-6121
207/948-2962